EAT FREE
OR DIE

by
Kevin Clemens

From the outside, the life of an
automotive journalist
seems like a dream. From the inside,
it could be murder

River's Bend Press
Stillwater, Minnesota

Eat Free or Die

Copyright © 2005 Kevin Clemens

First Edition

ISBN 0-9729445-3-2

Published by
River's Bend Press
Post Office Box 606
Stillwater, Minnesota 55082 USA
www.riversbendpress.com

Cover design by Sherry Wachter
Book design by Steven Semken

This is a work of fiction. Characters and corporations in this novel are either a product of the author's imagination, or if real, are used fictitiously without any intent to describe their past, present, or future conduct and activities. Any resemblance to actual events or locales, or persons living or dead, is entirely coincidental.

Library of Congress Cataloging-in-Publication Data
Clemens, Kevin, 1957-
  Eat free or die / by Kevin Clemens.— 1st trade pbk. ed.
    p. cm.
  ISBN 0-9729445-3-2 (trade pbk. : alk. paper)
  1. Automotive journalism--Fiction. 2. Journalists--Fiction. I. Title.
  PS3603.L458E18 2005
  813'.6--dc22
                        2005017137

For Loree, fittingly

PART I

"Never argue with anyone who buys
printer's ink by the barrel."
— H.L. Mencken

CHAPTER 1

The first glimmers of dawn were peeking over the sharp edge of the horizon. The Porsche's headlights illuminated several bleary-eyed people with towels and rags, wiping the dust from the flanks of the other sleek sports cars. Behind them, standing on a ladder, a man peered into the viewfinder of a camera mounted on a large heavy-duty tripod.

"Move the Mercedes back about a foot," he commanded into the radio gripped in his ungloved left hand.

The car started and everyone paused and watched while the big black coupe inched backward.

"That's it, hold it right there," came the crackling voice over the radio.

The towel holders resumed their polishing.

Simon St. Scot stood at the base of the ladder and stamped his feet to get warm. He was glad he'd brought his beat-up brown leather jacket. He flipped the collar up against the cold as his breath condensed into a cloud.

Photographers were always pulling this kind of thing: up before dawn, drive forty miles out into the stinking desert to some rock formation that looked just like any of the other rock formations closer to town, then an hour of moving cars this way and that until the rising sun provided enough light for shooting pictures; pictures that the magazine art director wouldn't like anyway; pictures that, in the end would get manipulated with a computer, placing the cars into a seascape or a mountain scene.

St. Scot began to doubt if shooting sunrises and sunsets was really necessary.

It was obscene to make everyone get up before dawn instead of sleeping in. They could have stayed out late the previous night and enjoyed a nice meal and a good bottle of wine at the magazine's expense. Instead, they cut the night short and now they were in the desert, at this ungodly hour of the morning, in search of the perfect shot. It was probably all a plot by photographers to exert their control over writers and magazine editors, St. Scot surmised. *Damn photographers.*

"Want to look?" asked Wayne Robbins, St. Scot's current tormentor. Robbins must have been in a really good mood. Photographers almost never let you look. He waited for Robbins to come down the ladder before clambering up beside the camera. The scene was dimly lit by the glow of the sun sitting just below the horizon, but St. Scot could see that Robbins knew his stuff. Arrayed in front of the lens were the Mercedes-Benz Coupe, a Ferrari, a Porsche and the new Jaguar sports car. Each was clearly visible in the frame along with some artistically arranged rocks and cacti in the edges of the composition. He scrambled down from the ladder and grunted something that sounded approving.

Moments later, Robbins was on top of the ladder again checking his light meter. *Thwack-flap.* The sound of the Nikon's shutter opening and closing filled the still air as Robbins took the first of the several hundred shots. Before the sun had fully appeared, the shoot was over.

As the senior staff person on this trip, it was St. Scot's unwritten and unspoken right to set the pace on the drive back to breakfast. Loafing along at 90-mph on the empty two-lane blacktop that stretched across the desert, he came to a long straightaway. Glancing over to see where the other cars were, he fingered the paddle shifters on the back of the Ferrari's steering wheel, banged it down two gears and stood on the gas. The snarl of the V-8 rose to a frantic scream as the red car rocketed across the landscape. A flick of his index finger on the back of the steering wheel and the car banged up a gear. He watched smugly in his mirrors as Jopp in the Porsche and Wright in the Mercedes reacted to his charge. Robbins and Hayward in the Jaguar were last in line and, with the photographer driving, were left far behind by the sudden burst of acceleration.

As the speedometer crossed 140-mph, St. Scot eased up on the throttle and flicked the paddle shifter back into top gear. The other two cars began to close and he waited until they reached him, holding his speed for another mile or two before gradually slowing back to his 90-mph cruising speed. Nothing like an early morning romp with an exotic Italian to put a smile on your face and the edge on your hunger for breakfast.

"You want hash browns, hon?"

St. Scot looked up into the inquiring face of Darlene, or at least that was what her Denny's nametag had written on it. He ordered hash browns, a three-egg mushroom omelet with rye toast, and a second glass of orange juice. It had been a good trip that would result in a cover story for *Motoring Magazine*, the magazine for which he worked. The cars were fabulous, the scenery was good (if you liked deserts), nothing had broken and nobody had crashed anything. That would make the new owners of the magazine happy.

St. Scot's job was to write about the Ferrari, the car he had gravitated to right from the start of the three-day drive. It was beautiful, of course. But more than that, it was built by people who understood how to perfectly blend racing cars with a car for the street. It was poetry. It was art. It had intensity. It was like having sex with a supermodel...

His lustful thoughts were interrupted by Darlene, bringing their food to the table. She stopped and looked out across the window into the parking lot.

"Are those your cars?" she asked wide-eyed.

"Why yes, yes they are," answered Haywood. "Want me to take you for a ride?" he said, with something approaching a pathetic leer.

Darlene looked torn for a second and then deflected Haywood's opening with, "My boyfriend has a Camaro and he would just die if he could see all of those cars."

The mushroom omelet on St. Scot's plate slowly soaked up the grease from the hash browns. He cut a piece of the artery putty with his fork and began eating.

It was clear that Haywood wasn't going to get anywhere. Darlene was cute enough: early twenties, thin blond hair and a slim figure in her Denny's outfit. She had a pretty smile. She had a very pretty smile. But what was Haywood thinking? They would be leaving in three hours. Ever since the guy had broken up with his girlfriend a few months earlier, he'd been hitting on every female he met. Women are good at sensing desperation. Haywood was three steps beyond that stage. Even St. Scot could see that.

Not that he was having much luck with romance himself. The problem was the job. The problem always had been and always would be the job. More than a dozen years earlier it had cost St. Scot his first marriage and, more recently, his second.

It was hard to build any sort of relationship when you were constantly flying off to Europe or Asia to drive fabulous cars and meet interesting people. Car companies flew you first class and put you in four-star hotels while wining and dining you at the world's most famous restaurants. Certainly it was a glamorous life and made you the envy of everyone at cocktail parties, so it seemed rather petty to whine about it, but it was a lonely type of existence. Over the course of his career, St. Scot had been to some of the world's most romantic locales—mostly in the company of a dozen other guys. Some of his male colleagues found that situation intriguing, but it wasn't a lifestyle choice that he wanted to embrace.

Sure, there were some women around, but female automotive writers were rare, and the ones who were part of the scene were savvy enough to avoid awkward entanglements with other writers. There were lots of women in the public relations departments of car companies, of course, but that would be a bit like sleeping with the enemy. His options were slim, and seemed to be getting slimmer.

St. Scot pulled himself out of this reverie, took out his corporate credit card and paid for the breakfast. Last night's hotel, a Four Seasons of enormous charm and grace, had already gone onto the card and so should have a very nice meal in a well-reviewed local restaurant. Instead, Robbins had them out past ten o'clock at night shooting sunset pictures in the desert...

Like most in his business, St. Scot fancied himself to be a gourmand and always looked forward to a really fine meal at a top restaurant, especially if (no not if, when) someone else was paying for it. But last night, like so many other times on the road...*Damn photographers.*

As he signed for the check, St. Scot made a mental note to get his monthly expense report in early, since that Four Season's bill would hit his statement hard. His personal monthly record was $17,000, but that included a two-day rental of a Ferrari in Los Angeles for a special event the publisher had wanted to do. You could never get rich being an automotive journalist, but you sure could live like you were.

St. Scot hated being late for anything and particularly hated rushing to make a plane. Traveling with a laptop computer always meant even longer-than-usual delays going through security, so he liked to make sure he had plenty of time, even if it meant sitting around in the departure lounge or airline club. Robbins, on the other hand, prided himself on his ability to make airplanes by the narrowest of margins. Today the photographer had milked the time for some more shots for all it was worth and now the whole crew was dashing up to the ticket counter, only to find that their flight would be delayed for at least a half an hour. Robbins looked at St. Scot smugly, as though he had once again cheated time and come out the winner.

St. Scot ignored him and, instead, pulled out his cell phone to check his voicemail. He hated cell phones and never left his turned on, much to the despair of the magazine's overworked Managing Editor, Mark Summers.

Summers was high-strung and nervous all the time and he had an ability to make even the calmest people around him feel the same way. He lived in permanent fear that he was going to be fired at any moment. The nervousness was infectious and soon everyone figured Summers was about to get the axe. Even the upper management at the magazine would occasionally question why Summers was still around and why they hadn't fired him months ago. This caused nearly constant rumors among the staff that the Managing Editor was about to be fired, which, of course, fueled his further anxiety.

Even though Summers made every kind of threat he could think of to St. Scot about leaving his phone on, St. Scot knew he didn't really have enough clout to make him change his evil cell-phone ignoring ways. Besides, he'd heard a rumor that Summers was about to be fired.

St. Scot checked his messages. Three calls from Summers asking him to call in as soon as he could. He ignored these. Next, there was a call from Elizabeth Meyers. Meyers Communications was a major player with an automotive client who wanted to make sure there was a "car guy" in their Public Relations firm. He knew that Elizabeth had more or less promised that she could get a senior editor from one of the big magazines to join her happy staff and she'd set her sights on him. At first her flunkies had made the calls but now, because St. Scot hadn't been as willing to roll over for the dough, she was making the calls herself. She had been trying to entice St. Scot away from his automotive journalism job and to join the dark side of corporate Public Relations for some time now. Many of his colleagues had already gone over and were pulling down salaries five times what they had as magazine writers. Almost to a person they had been changed by the switch, becoming corporate suits, leaving behind their reasoning power and their humanity. It paid a lot of money and all you really had to do was sell your soul.

St. Scot shuddered.

He listened to her message again.

They had once been, what?

Together?

No.

An item?

No.

Lovers?

Ah, yes, that was the word.

St. Scot figured Elizabeth Meyers would continue to court him to join her firm for another two weeks before she would give up on him and try to find another editor to coax to the dark side. He thought of the smell of her long silky auburn hair and the ample curves of her luscious body for several long seconds and then ignored her call, too.

The last call on Simon St. Scot's answering voicemail would change his life. It was from Blinsky.

CHAPTER 2

St. Scot glanced out the window of the jumbo jet. At 37,000 feet the permanently snow-covered peaks of the Rocky Mountains are impressive. Rising almost halfway up to an airliner's cruising altitude they are at once hostile and barren, and yet strangely inviting. You could get lost out there. No deadlines, no Public Relations firms, no managing editors, no cell phones and no damn photographer s. St. Scot slumped into his coach class seat and for the hundredth time tried to figure out what Blinsky had meant in his phone message.

Ivan Rachmaninov Blinsky lived in Vienna. Despite his overtly Russian name, Blinsky was an American whose mother had married a dry-cleaner from New Jersey. Their union produced an only child who, in a fit of parental Jewish rage against McCarthyism, was christened with his unlikely and unfortunate name. Growing up, Ivan was taunted mercilessly for his bizarre moniker. He had no friends. At Columbia University, he displayed such dubious aptitude that they asked him to stay an extra year to earn his Bachelor's of Arts degree in Russian studies. He grew a goatee and learned to perfect a nearly flawless accent so that he could pass himself off as a Russian count, which proved irresistible to the art girls who wore only black

9

and populated much of New York City. He couldn't actually speak Russian, of course, so when his acquaintances would bring real Russians for him to converse with, Blinsky used his commanding and imperious position as a Russian count to insist that they speak only English while they were visiting America. After some time impersonating a Russian count, Blinsky realized that, while he was sleeping with lots of art history and English majors, there wasn't any real money in the ruse and decided to get a job.

Somehow, without friends in high places (or even friends in low places), or any experience as a journalist, or credentials in the auto industry, Blinsky convinced the *Montreal Post Dispatch* to send him on permanent assignment to Vienna. His beat was reporting on the emerging auto industry in the countries that made up the former Soviet Union. The editors at the *Dispatch* figured having a Russian count, practically an insider, would be just the thing.

The funny thing was Blinsky turned out to have a real ability to make up interesting stories. They were complete fiction and total fabrications, but, when one of his fictitious stories ran, more often than not it would be confirmed a few weeks later by other news reporters who had actually gone to the source. There were grumblings that he was simply being fed information by the former KGB, the Russian Mafia or perhaps space aliens. Regardless, Blinsky developed a reputation as one of the leading lights of the industry. Because the newspaper paid him a livable wage (and mostly because Austrian women were vigorous in their sexual curiosity toward foreign men) it was almost a better scam than being a displaced Russian count in New York.

It was St. Scot who had followed up one of Blinsky's stories about a new car that was being built by a consortium of former Russian industrialists in Turkmenistan. After Blinsky broke the story, the Russians decided to invite a select number of top American journalists to the shores of the Caspian Sea to drive the new car. It was a trip organized to provide background material for future stories, but its real purpose was for the Russians to find out from the American journalists how their car would fare on the U.S. market and, more importantly, to buy some journalistic goodwill for the launch of the car. St. Scot had reached a high enough level in the hierarchy of his magazine to attend the executive level trip, and was among those who were wined and dined. The caviar had been the finest Beluga. There had been seven different kinds of vodka; all of it served ice-cold. There had also been a bevy of very beautiful "administrative assistants," none of whom were served ice-cold, and it was made very clear that any one or more of them would be happy to share the beds of any of the journalists. Few slept alone in the cold desert air that night. St. Scot had. He had thought he was there to give feedback about the car. He had been brutally honest with the Russians and they hadn't been happy to hear his criticisms of the car's shortcomings.

The damn thing was just crude and there was no way around it. You couldn't even compare it to a Honda or even a Hyundai and he didn't hesitate to say so, figuring it was better to let the executives know in private than to read his bad reviews when the car hit the market a couple of years later down the line. He realized, too late, he should have kept his mouth shut and slept with a pair of the delicious Russian tarts. The executives thanked him coldly and sent him back home with a reminder that everything was strictly confidential and embargoed so nothing could be written about the company until the launch of the new car. The last St. Scot had heard, two of the Russian "executives" had been killed in gangland style hits by their Russian Mafia colleagues and the whole company had gone belly up.

St. Scot met Blinsky shortly after the Caspian Sea boondoggle, on a Volvo press trip in Norway. Car companies occasionally invite journalists to the most outlandish places they can think of. The more ordinary and pedestrian the automobile, the more bizarre the destination. In this case, the place was a tiny village called Kirkenness, far to the north of the Arctic Circle and actually closer to the North Pole than it is to Norway's capital city of Oslo. Since the trip took place in December, the region was in total darkness for twenty-two hours a day, the remaining two hours filled with a misty gray light that seemed to brighten a bit at around one in the afternoon.

Just getting to the place was a trial. St. Scot had flown from the U.S. into London. From there he took a flight to Copenhagen where a privately chartered jet awaited the journalists. The flight from Copenhagen to Kirkenness took several hours over a barren and snow-covered landscape that was barely visible in the gloomy winter half-light of the far north. Finally, arriving in the early afternoon under a pitch black sky, the journalists were bussed to the premiere hotel in Kirkenness—a simple place that reminded St. Scot of a Holiday Inn near a discount ski resort. The rooms were plain and most had a chaste pair of twin beds. It wasn't the Ritz, but then this wasn't Paris. There might have been a revolt over the quality of the accommodations among some of the more snobbish auto writers, but that unpleasantness was averted when Volvo announced that the hotel bar was open and drinks were on the house. It may have only been 2 p.m., but the nighttime sky said "Happy Hour" to the press corps.

Kirkenness had withstood the second heaviest bombing of any city during World War II. The Germans had built several airbases there to intercept and bomb supply ships heading for the port of Murmansk in Russia. British, Russian and American bombers flew mission after mission from Murmansk, literally bombing Kirkenness into the ground in an attempt to wipe out the German air bases. The inhabitants lived through most of the war in the large iron mines under the city. Having survived this terrible ordeal, they were fairly certain they could survive an influx of European and American motoring journalists overrunning their city. They should have locked up more of their liquor.

Driving the Volvos in the dark over snow-covered roads around Kirkenness would prove very little about how the cars would perform in Santa Monica or Dayton. But the place was so outrageous, it was a guarantee that being invited to this outpost at the end of the Earth would result in a story that would make other journalists jealous; always a top goal for a successful automotive writer.

The Volvo press department devised an itinerary for the journalists that included a quick drive around the coast road. This road provided a view of the former evil-empire of Russia, across the river that formed the border with Norway. The plan was to then spend a couple of hours playing with the cars on an ice track before returning to Kirkenness for dinner. As luck would have it (or perhaps not have it), St. Scot was paired with Blinsky in an all-wheel drive wagon with an automatic transmission. Having never met, he figured Blinsky was just another European automotive journalist. He certainly had the act down: arrogant, demanding, whining about everything in his thick foreign accent, like so many other Euro-trash writers St. Scot had met on other such trips.

The morning of the event, they left the hotel with St. Scot driving into the murky darkness. Blinsky was pouring over the maps that Volvo had thoughtfully provided in case any of the journalists got lost.

After a couple of miles of silence Blinsky suddenly announced "My family's ancestral castle is very near by. Turn left up ahead and we will go and visit there!"

St. Scot was a bit uneasy about deviating from the route that Volvo's press department had carefully planned for them just so some Russian count could visit his old family castle, especially when the road Blinsky wanted him to take led straight to the Russian border. But Blinsky repeated his instruction and St. Scot surprised himself by quickly obeying. *How could he refuse a command from a Russian count?*

As their station wagon slowly approached the closed barricades at the border, the hair on St. Scot's neck stood on end. Two guards with Kalashnikov machine guns were standing in the pools of harsh electric lighting at the entrance to the guard shack, watching with interest as the car approached. St. Scot fingered his passport in the pocket of his down jacket. *Were Americans allowed to simply drive into Russia? Did Russian counts have diplomatic immunity that allowed them to bring guests in and out of the country? Would a Volvo's windshield stop a round from a Kalashnikov?*

The car rolled to a stop in front of the lowered gate. As one of the guards walked toward them, St. Scot rolled down his electric window. The guard barked something to him in Russian. St. Scot tried to smile and pointed to Blinsky. The other guard now walked over to the passenger side of the car and motioned Blinsky to roll down his window. He did so slowly with an imperious air that spoke volumes about his royal Russian lineage. The second guard, apparently taken aback by the calm demeanor of the person before him, quietly and with great deference asked Blinsky something in Russian. Blinsky nodded his head slowly.

He then picked up the open map from his lap and turned to the guard, and spoke in his best New Jersey accent, "Hey there!" he began, gesturing to himself and St. Scot. "We're two Americans from Atlantic City, New Jersey and I think we're lost. Is this the way to the Arctic Ocean?"

Later, after the guards had lowered their machine guns, after St. Scot had convinced them that they really were lost American tourists, after they had given the Russians all of their bottled water and chewing gum, Volvo press kits and the Volvo owner's manual out of the glove box, along with all of Blinsky's Turkish cigarettes, they were allowed to carefully turn the Volvo around and head back the way they'd come.

"You know?" said Blinsky, "right up until that guard spoke to me, I actually thought we were going to pull it off."

Blinsky had dropped the Russian accent and kept talking like the guy from New Jersey he really was. A safe distance from the border gate St. Scot pulled the car to the side of the road and slowly turned to face Blinsky.

"What would you have done if they had started shooting at us?" he asked.

Blinsky frowned for a moment before replying "I really hadn't thought that far ahead."

If that brush with absurdity and danger hadn't sealed their relationship, what came next did. That afternoon they arrived at the ice-driving course that Volvo had set up on a small frozen pond. The course was in the shape of an oval and the object was to test the traction capability of their new all-wheel drive system. In the center of the oval was a small island littered with rocks and small trees. St. Scot drove first, sliding the car in graceful arcs around the island, the Volvo sedan never pointing exactly forward but always sliding in the proper direction. St. Scot was proud of his car control skills and this ice rink was the perfect opportunity for him to show off. After several laps of displaying his virtuosity, during which time Blinsky was quietly watching from the passenger seat with rapt attention, St. Scot slid the car expertly to the edge of the track. They switched seats and Blinsky carefully adjusted his seat position and mirrors before gently driving onto the track.

He then accelerated hard, fully demonstrating the car's superior all-wheel drive traction on slippery surfaces. When he got to the first corner, he didn't lift his foot off the gas. He didn't turn the steering wheel. He watched with an unblinking stare as the Volvo hurtled toward the dirt embankment that marked the edge of the ice pond. St. Scot immediately understood that he couldn't do anything but sink into his seat and trust that Volvo's engineers had done their sums right when they'd designed the car's seatbelts. As they flew headlong toward the embankment he scanned his mind back to the videos of Volvo crash testing and tried to remember how well the cars had done with frontal impacts.

They hit the dirt bank with a glancing blow, spinning them back across the ice. Blinsky's foot was still firmly planted on the gas pedal and the grip of the winter tires and all-wheel drive helped the car accelerate smartly across the ice as it approached the small island. For an instant St. Scot thought if everything went well they would hit a rock or a tree and the car would come to a grinding stop. Everything didn't go well. The car hit a couple of small rocks first before striking a half-buried log and rolling several times. Both men were tossed around, but the safety systems, in apparent anticipation that a total idiot would someday drive the car, protected them from any injury. The car ended upside down at the edge of the island. Blinsky looked at St. Scot hanging from his seatbelts. He looked perplexed.

Finally, with the most sincere expression possible while hanging upside down in his seatbelt, he said to St. Scot, "Damn, I almost had it. What do you think I did wrong?"

There were no consequences for Blinsky to face. He had wrecked a press car. So what? He had done it before. Nobody cared. They could make more of them. The greatest concern for the Volvo people was that nobody was hurt and that Blinsky wasn't blaming the car for the accident. There was lots of talk about treacherous conditions and worn tires. There was never any suggestion that Blinsky didn't have a clue how to drive.

When they got back to the hotel in Kirkenness, Blinsky went straight to the bar so that he could tell his tale of daring-do. And with each telling of the story, his own superb driving skills were magnified while the abilities of the Volvo wagon to handle ice and snow were questioned. By dinnertime, Blinsky was running on pure alcohol and the ancestry of the Volvo PR people was coming into question. By this time he had reverted back to his native Russian persona and a number of his European colleagues came up to congratulate him on his escape from sure death, and on his having saved the life of an American journalist.

That evening, in the finest automotive press trip tradition, Volvo took over a restaurant and laid out a feast. The room they were in was paneled in cedar and a cozy fire crackled in the fireplace at one end. The warmth of the room, the pleasant aroma of the cedar mixed with the smell of the burning wood, along with the vestiges of jet lag, made everyone very mellow. Long tables with white tablecloths flanked a center buffet that was set with foods from the region. There was fish. Lots of fish. Boiled fish. Baked Fish. Pickled fish. Fish garnished with fish. The Norwegians like fish. There were lots of potatoes and strange salads made from bits of vegetable and fish suspended in Jell-O. For those who were tired of fish, there was reindeer meat. For dessert there were cloudberries and lingonberries on pudding. There was lots of alcohol, served by smiling rosy-cheeked blond Norwegian girls and by a black-haired Lapp woman whose soft dark eyes told a man that she knew more about him than he knew about himself. The ancestry of the Volvo PR people was now being praised. St. Scot had a few bruises and felt sore from his ride with Blinsky, who had made it a point to carefully avoid him for the rest of the trip.

St. Scot would have been perfectly happy to have left things like that, but for some reason, ever since that press trip above the Arctic Circle, Blinsky assumed that he and St. Scot were now the best of pals. Routinely, St. Scot would receive faxes and e-mails about arcane technical details of cars that had been built in the thirties. He would receive requests for tune-up information for six-cylinder Chevrolet engines of the fifties. None of it ever made any sense. If his phone rang in the middle of the night, he was pretty certain that it was Blinsky wanting to share something unusual or frightening or ridiculous. After a while, St. Scot didn't mind so much. It was like having a crazy uncle living in your attic—and the attic was in Vienna, thousands of miles away.

But this most recent message from Blinsky on St. Scot's answering machine came as a shock.

CHAPTER 3

"**P**ick me up at the airport tomorrow night. I am going to be your new boss."

That was all. No Russian accent either. What did it mean? *Motoring Magazine* was going through some major changes since the founders, Bob and Zelda Fisher, had sold out. After twenty-five years, the last of the publishing world's true independents was gobbled up by the bean counters at Worldwide Publications Incorporated, known as WPI.

WPI had offices in New York, Europe and Asia and holdings that included television networks, newspapers and insurance companies. The business press occasionally linked the company to new ventures in Russia and the former Soviet States. It was mostly a huge, faceless, multi-national corporation whose properties were expected to make good profits. Bob and Zelda had met with the staff the day before the sale was finalized and assured everyone that the family atmosphere they had fostered would remain; no one would be fired and everything would be business as usual. That was eighteen months ago and business as usual was no longer the name of the game.

Good profits in the magazine business come from high advertising revenue. Saying bad things about people who advertise in your magazine is not usually a route to keeping the advertisers happy and there was already pressure being applied to moderate editorial content. If a story was written with a disparaging remark about the antiquated engines used by a certain domestic automotive manufacturer in one of its carry-over models, by the time the magazine hit the newsstands the comments would be gone. Somebody at WPI was changing the copy before the magazine was ready to go to print. The editorial staff complained, of course, but management had the final say, claiming that a last minute ad placement had caused the story to be shortened; that the cut had nothing to do with content. The staff knew better but felt their hands were tied. They worried about what other changes lay ahead.

Sitting in his window seat on the airplane, St. Scot tried to work out when Blinsky would be arriving. He hadn't said which flight he would be coming in on or what time he might arrive. Spotting the Air Phone located in the seatback in front of him, St. Scot slid his well-worn corporate credit card through the slot and dialed the magazine's office number.

As soon as the phone was answered, St. Scot knew something was wrong. Instead of the pleasant and familiar voice of Maryanne Acres, the cheerful middle-aged receptionist who had been with the magazine from its inception, a sullen male voice answered the phone "Worldwide Publications Incorporated."

"Yes, this is Simon St. Scot. I'd like to speak with Terrance Filby."

"He is no longer employed here," the male voice responded.

St. Scot stared at the phone. *Terry gone? How? He was the only editor-in-chief the magazine had ever known, for Christ's sake!*

"Well, let me speak with William Borgenson then…"

"That guy is gone too," came the reply.

Filby and Borgenson both gone? Did he still have a job?

"Let me speak with Mark Summers," St. Scot commanded.

There was a click and some static before St. Scot heard the phone ringing.

"Hello?"

It was Summers' twitchy, nervous voice.

"Mark, what the hell is going on?" demanded St. Scot.

"As if you didn't know!" came the angry reply.

"What do you mean by that? Tell me what's happening!" he said.

"About an hour ago Winston Marshfield from WPI came here with three security guards and called everyone into the conference room. He told us that changes were needed and that he was there to make them."

Summers voice was beginning to crack.

"Marshfield then told Terry and Bill that they were both fired. Just like that. Assigned a guard to each of them and told them to clean out their desks and to be out of the building in fifteen minutes. It was as if they were being led off like prisoners."

St. Scot looked out the window at the rolling plains far below the aircraft.

"Who else?" asked St. Scot.

"Marshfield told Maryanne and Betty to clean out their desks, too," replied Summers.

Betty Waltrip was Terrance Filby's executive secretary. St. Scot was afraid to ask the next question. He paused for a moment.

"Do I still have a job, Mark?"

There was an even longer pause before Summers replied in a low, controlled voice.

"What the hell do you mean, Simon? Winston Marshfield told us that if we had any questions we should talk to you. That the changes were all your idea..."

"My God, Mark, this is insanity! Call the staff together and we'll meet first thing Monday morning." He then hung up the phone and sat staring out the window.

It was early evening when St. Scot's flight touched down. He hurried through the terminal and hopped aboard the FlyRight parking shuttle that took him to one of the outer commercial parking lots. A new Lexus sedan was waiting for him. It had been delivered earlier that day with a full tank of gas and would be his ride for the weekend. With over 600 car and truck nameplates and models on the market it was clearly impossible to drive everything each year, so car companies went to great effort to make their vehicles available for journalists to drive. Few in the automotive journalism profession even bothered owning their own cars, since press vehicles were always available. Going on a trip with the family? Borrow a minivan from Chrysler. Moving? Get a GMC pickup truck. Got a hot date? That Porsche will do just fine. Going to your high school reunion? Got to be a Ferrari.

The Lexus was smooth, powerful and supremely comfortable. St. Scot settled in for the twenty minute drive to his home. He arrived in front of a dilapidated red brick firehouse, got out and put his key into a shiny new padlock hanging on one of the huge front doors. Stepping inside, the smell of canvas and oil and leather and gasoline mixed together to form an aroma that never failed to please him. He punched his code into the alarm system, turned back to swing open the heavy door and drove the Lexus to a parking spot next to a huge vehicle that was draped with a car cover. Surrounding him in the dimly lit building were several other carefully covered vehicles.

He had purchased the 100-year old fire station six years earlier, when the city declared it obsolete. St. Scot purchased it from the city with money that had been left to him by his parents. Its weathered red brick façade fit in well with the slightly rundown character of the neighborhood in which it was situated. St. Scot had employed a crew of workmen to renovate the second floor, creating a loft for his own living space. With three bedrooms, a full-size and very complete kitchen and a small but cozy living area, St. Scot loved his self-made refuge; particularly the brass fireman's pole at one end of the living room (although he'd added a thick gymnastics pad at the bottom, after a young woman he was especially trying to impress broke her ankle late one night). On the main level, St. Scot had painted the cracked concrete floor with a gray, two-part epoxy that resisted the occasional oil drips and fluid stains from his collection of classic cars. He had also installed overhead lights and an alarm system to make it easier to work on more than one project at a time and to keep things secure during his frequent trips away from home. The thing that meant the most to him, however, was the building's link to the past. The firehouse had seen the transition from horse-drawn fire wagons all the way through modern pumpers and ladder trucks, and every time he unlocked its big front doors he could imagine the men of Engine Company No. 7 rushing off to put out a fire, save a child from drowning or rescuing somebody's kitten from a tree.

St. Scot pulled the door shut, padlocked it again and went around to the front door of the building where he let himself in with his key. He climbed the stairs to his loft and, glancing at the answering machine on the kitchen counter, saw that the red message light was blinking. The first message was from Elizabeth Meyers. It was short and to the point.

"Simon, I don't think we have a place in our organization for you after all. Certain information has been made available to me that will make it impossible for Meyers Communications to consider you for employment. Goodbye, Simon."

St. Scot hit the pause button. What the hell was this about? Certain information? What information? He hadn't wanted the job, but he also wanted to make sure he refused it on his own terms. *Now this?* In all the time he had known her, he could never remember her sounding so cold. Even when their relationship had ended, she hadn't sounded that cold. He hit the resume button.

The second message was from Terrance Filby. The old man sounded agitated and drunk.

"You bastard! You filthy bastard! You couldn't wait your turn. You had to dump your friends to get ahead. Well, you have no friends anymore, not in this industry. You may still have your job, but I am going to make it my life's work to make the world know that you're nothing more than a washed-up toady!"

St. Scot quickly hit the pause button again. His head was reeling. This was like a bad dream. He had worked for Filby for twelve years. He looked up to him as a mentor and tried to pattern his professional career after the great man's life. Terry and Barbara had treated him like an adopted son. No, this was not a dream. This was a nightmare.

What the hell was going on?

Reluctantly he hit the resume button again. The message was from Blinsky.

"Simon, where are you? This isn't the way to impress your new boss. I'm at the airport and you haven't picked me up. I guess I'll take a taxi to the Hilton. Call me when you get this message. We have a lot of work to do to whip that rag of a magazine into shape and we need to get started."

St. Scot hit the rewind button and listened to the message again. There was no mistake. It was the second time that Blinsky had said he was St. Scot's new boss. *What the hell was going on?*

There was only one way to find out. St. Scot headed for the garage. He was going to drive out to see his new boss, a certain Ivan Rachmaninov Blinsky.

CHAPTER 4

The Hilton's elevator whisked St. Scot to the eleventh floor. He had called Blinsky's room ahead of time and had been informed by some male voice that Mr. Blinsky was in a meeting, but that St. Scot should come up to the suite on the executive level and wait. The elevator was glass and stainless steel construction and looked as cold and sterile as the rest of the hotel. Modern, clean and efficient, but lacking the charm and grace that the truly great hotels of the world possess.

St. Scot rode alone and in silence. Apparently they shut off the elevator music after a certain time in the evening. Or maybe the hotel was too classy for Muzak. In its place he quietly hummed *What kind of fool am I?* to himself.

St. Scot knocked on the door of the suite. A well-dressed young man in a blue blazer and tie answered the door. St. Scot identified himself, and the man led him into the sitting room located between the suite's bedroom and corporate meeting area. Some non-descript, bulk-purchased artwork graced the walls and there were two half-empty coffee cups on a small table in front of the chair to which St. Scot was led. From behind the closed door to the conference room he could hear the murmur of voices. Suddenly, the door opened and Blinsky stuck his head out.

"Ah, Simon. It's about time. Come in here, please. I want you to meet the new team that is going to turn your sinking ship around and get it back on track."

St. Scot ignored the badly mixed metaphor and followed Blinsky into the conference room.

"Gentlemen," he said, "I want you to meet my right hand man, Simon St. Scot."

Seated at a conference table cluttered with coffee cups and half-eaten sandwiches were a bunch of suits. St. Scot recognized them immediately as the types who ran most huge publishing empires. They wouldn't know a good story if they were sitting on it. They had little time for the artistic side of the business. Writers were their production workers, screwing together the product. The magazine was just a means of getting advertising into the hands of the reader. These execs lived and breathed New York City and, to them, cars were yellow and black and had Taxi written on them. If they could make money by producing magazines that appealed to car enthusiasts that was all they cared to know about the actual machines.

Winston Marshfield sat at the head of the table. He was in his mid-forties and had a head of distinguished-looking silver hair. His blue eyes held St. Scot in an intense stare. Next to him was Roland Beeson, the finance guy at WPI. Beeson was a pudgy little thirty-something guy who was beginning to suffer from male-pattern baldness. He hadn't reached the comb-over stage yet, but it was clear that it was only a matter of time. Beeson had visited the magazine office a month before and couldn't resist pointing out places where the editors and staff could save money on everything from paper towels in the bathroom to gasoline in the press cars. He had actually suggested that they carpool on test drives to save money. *What an idiot.*

There were three other men in the room: an Asian about the same age as Marshfield and two others who were Beeson's age and looked like they might be Slavic. Nobody rose, nobody was introduced and nobody offered to shake hands. There was a tense silence in the room. Blinsky awkwardly tried to fill it.

"As you gentlemen know, I asked you specifically to keep Simon as my assistant. He and I have a long friendship and have worked together in the past," Blinsky said.

St. Scot searched his memory for any indication that either of those statements might be true. *Nope. Not a word of it.*

Marshfield interrupted abruptly, "Our business is finished. Goodbye."

He rose from his chair, gathered the papers that had been before him, stared pointedly at St. Scot for several long seconds and walked out of the room. The rest of the assembled suits stood as one and followed him. Their precision and timing was exquisite. If they had been a drill team, St. Scot would have applauded them.

St. Scot stood where he was, only now looking Blinsky squarely in the face. There had been some changes since he had seen him last. The goatee was gone, as was any pretense of being a Russian count. He was wearing an expensive suit and St. Scot recognized the handiwork of a Seville Row tailor. His tie was from Ferragamo and his shoes were Italian. Without the goatee, his face seemed wider and his eyes more bulging. He had put on a few pounds, no doubt due to all the butter-cream tortes served in every coffeehouse in Vienna.

"What the hell is going on, Ivan?" St. Scot's calm voice betrayed an anger that seethed below the surface.

Blinsky placed a hand on St. Scot's shoulder and motioned for him to sit down. St. Scot took the seat that Beeson had occupied while Blinsky sat in Marshfield's seat. Symbolic. Blinsky leaned back in the chair and put his hands behind his head. For several seconds he held this pose, controlling the situation, and then he leaned forward and looked St. Scot directly in the eyes.

"Simon," he started, "ever since that day in Norway I have enjoyed your friendship. You have been so helpful to me and have taught me so much about this wonderful business."

St. Scot tried to think of how tune-up instructions for a fifties Chevrolet six-cylinder engine might have helped Blinsky in the business.

"Now I have been granted a fabulous opportunity to change the automotive industry, and who better to join me but my good friend Simon St. Scot." Blinsky was getting excited now and beginning to revert to his faux-Russian speech patterns.

"You know, they wanted to get rid of you, too, when they canned Filby and Borgenson. But I convinced them that I needed you to implement the changes and keep the place going. I told them you and I were cut from the same cloth and that we would be able to build a well-oiled machine out of the disaster that Fishers left behind."

St. Scot's anger started to rise. *Who the hell was this Ruskie to run down all that he and his friends had built for more than a decade?*

"You know they picked me because I am such a genuine institution in the automotive industry," Blinsky continued. "A genius, really, in analyzing trends and predicting the future. They practically begged me to come back to America and help straighten out not only the magazine, but the entire auto industry."

Blinsky sat in front of St. Scot looking righteous and noble, which, with his years of training as a Russian count, he did very well.

St. Scot was about to open his mouth and tear apart the pompous jerk when the young man from the outer room opened the door and spoke, "The jet is leaving in fifteen minutes. Mr. Marshfield said that if you aren't on it you'll be left behind."

In one swift movement, Blinsky was up from his chair and bolting for the door, shouting over his shoulder, "I'll call you tomorrow from New York. Meanwhile, think of how we can increase circulation."

The door slammed shut and St. Scot was left sitting alone in the conference room, trying to make sense out of what had just happened. The more he thought about it, the madder he got. *Who did they think he was? What was it Filby had called him? A washed-up toady?* St. Scot stood and left the deserted suite for the elevator. He didn't feel like singing this time. Suddenly, the three-day test drive in the desert, the photo shoot and the flight home were beginning to catch up with him. Exhausted, he eased the Lexus out of the parking lot and turned it toward home. Tomorrow he would find out from Filby what was really going on.

CHAPTER 5

The next morning, St. Scot drove to Filby's house in his MGA. The 1950s roadster wasn't terribly fast, but it had a delightful vintage aura that always made him feel dashing, a bit like Cary Grant driving Grace Kelly's Sunbeam Talbot in *To Catch a Thief*. It was one of Barbara's favorite cars and he hoped it would remind her that they had been friends for a long time, like family even. Today he would see if he had been disowned.

It was a beautiful sunny day and the ten minutes to the bagel shop and then the fifteen minutes to the Filby's had gone by too quickly. He hadn't had enough time to plan what he was going to say. It turned out he didn't need to.

Almost as soon as he rolled to a stop, the front door opened and Terry charged out to meet him.

"You have a lot of nerve showing up here!" he shouted. "Get out of here you traitor, get out before I call the cops!"

Barbara walked out of the doorway and said over her husband's rantings, "You will do no such thing. Simon, there's got to be more to the story. Terry, let him come inside and explain his side before you hang him from a tree. Anyway, you can always chase him off later with your shotgun."

Barbara's logic appeared to carry the day and Terry stood back to let St. Scot exit his low slung roadster.

Simon followed Filby into the house and through a maze of dimly lit corridors. The rooms were decorated with the wonderful artifacts that a lifetime of travel seems to generate. Filby was born in the English Midlands, he'd gone to the best public schools in England before finally ending up at Oxford. His interests in politics and current events lead him to a career as a documentary filmmaker before switching to the magazine business. He had run several big news magazines in New York before leaving to indulge in his passion for classic cars.

His collection was impressive and nearly all of his cars were ready to drive at a moment's notice. He kept his favorite ten or so cars in a garage situated behind his house, while the rest were kept in a climate-controlled warehouse and automotive restoration shop that had been built to his own specifications. Mort Welsh, his British mechanic, worked on the collection daily to keep everything in top condition. Filby had managed to buy the right cars at the right time, just before the classic car boom of the late 1980s. Some of the cars he owned had increased in value by a factor of ten or more. Some by much more. Filby moved in the elite circle of collectors whose cars almost never went up for auction; cars quietly passed from one collector to another for stratospheric prices and were never shown to the public.

If Filby were to sell his entire collection, he would no doubt be a very wealthy man. But that option seemed to have no interest for him. He had sold some of his best cars when prices had been at their highest and used the money to acquire even more classic cars. It was said that his main reason for collecting was that it gave him access to men of genuine influence and power, and he wasn't about to throw that away for something as unimportant as mere money. Most speculated that the same held true with the magazine.

It was generally accepted that Filby ran the magazine because he enjoyed it and because it gave him a chance to pal around with the guys who ran the car companies. Under the new management of WPI, however, Filby hadn't seemed all that happy. The Fishers had let him be the captain of his ship, running it in whichever way he wanted it to go. But with WPI, Filby was no more or less important than any of the other dozen or so magazine editors on the payroll, and it seemed to him as though his ideas and perceptions were sought less and less frequently by the group of thirty-something bean counters who ran the publications section of the multi-national conglomerate.

In addition to granting Filby financial independence, his car collection had, on occasion, also provided a positive effect on St. Scot's income. For a time he had moonlighted for Terry, authenticating some of the more important cars in the collection as well as writing the histories of specific cars into special hand-tooled, leather-bound volumes, enhancing a car's value in this rarefied market. St. Scot was well-paid for this work, but had had to swear to Terry that he wouldn't tell anyone about the cars he had chronicled. After awhile, he'd become too busy with travel at the magazine and Bill Borgenson took over the task.

Simon and Filby entered a bright sunroom at the back of the house overlooking a small, but well-tended, flower garden. Barbara had already set out three placemats with knives and plates on a wrought iron and glass table. Terry looked at her and raised his eyebrows. Barbara just smiled and gestured to the men to sit down. She then opened the bag of warm bagels and passed them around. The three sat in silence, studiously spreading the cream cheese on the bagels. Finally, Terry could hold himself back no longer.

"Why did you do it, Simon? Why did you sell every one of us down the river?" he demanded.

St. Scot put his bagel down on his plate. He had been trying all night to think of what he wanted to say to Terry and Barbara.

"I don't know what is going on," he began. "I was on the sports car trip in the desert and when I came back, you and Bill and Maryanne and Betty were all fired. I didn't know anything about it. You have to believe me. I thought the Fishers had arranged it so that we would work together after WPI took over. Now this happens and somebody is hanging it on me. Terry, you know me. You tell me, what's going on."

Filby looked at St. Scot skeptically before he answered.

"Listen, why would Marshfield suddenly tell everyone that you had masterminded the whole thing, that you were the one pulling the strings and getting rid of people so that you could run the magazine, if it weren't true?"

St. Scot felt his stomach lurch. "The first I heard about any of this was when I got a phone call from Ivan Blinsky!" St. Scot replied.

Filby's face darkened.

"Blinsky! That idiot? He couldn't find his ass with both hands! Are you saying he is the mastermind behind all of this?

That's absurd! If that's the best you can do, take your bagels and get out," Filby shouted, glowering at St. Scot.

St. Scot tried to think of something to say. He started slowly pacing his words, trying to stay calm.

"Terry, how has the magazine been doing since WPI took over?" he asked.

Filby looked at St. Scot suspiciously and answered carefully.

"We've been doing okay," he began, "but not as well as we had been under Bob and Zelda. That's to be expected, of course. It always takes some time for the bugs to get worked out…"

Filby let the sentence hang there for a minute.

Then he added, "If you're suggesting that Bill and I were part of the reason for that, you're wrong! In fact, we had a meeting less than a month ago with Marshfield where we presented plans to bring the magazine right up to number one!"

Filby had a fire in his eye.

"And we would have done it if it hadn't been for your backstabbing," he added under his breath.

St. Scot was about to reply when the phone next to Barbara rang. She answered it and immediately went pale. Her eyes looked frightened and both of the men waited until she had finished. When she hung up she turned to them and said, "That was Helen. Bill is dead. Suicide, they think. Helen is there with the police and she wants us to come over right away."

Stunned, they hurriedly piled into Terry's big GMC Suburban and drove to Bill and Helen Borgenson's house. The Borgenson's lived on a small tract of land that used to be a farm. Helen had renovated the house with modern appliances to make it more comfortable, while still retaining its charming farmhouse character. Bill had rebuilt the old barn into a combination work studio and shop where he could work on his hobby of taxidermy. He had insulated the walls and ceiling, put in windows and skylights and installed a heat pump to provide air conditioning and heat.

When St. Scot, Terry and Barbara arrived at the house they were met by a woman who introduced herself as Bill and Helen's next door neighbor. She was a strong-looking older woman who had clearly seen her share of tragedy.

"Helen's been given a sedative and is lying down," she said.

Barbara went upstairs to see if she could comfort her friend while Terry and St. Scot got the story from the neighbor woman.

"I was at dinner with Bill and Helen last night," she started. "We had stroganoff and I brought cobbler for dessert…" she trailed off.

"Do you think Bill was especially angry or even despondent over losing his job yesterday?" Filby asked, while glaring at St. Scot.

"No, no, not particularly," she said, looking thoughtful. "In fact he said that this might be the best thing that ever happened to him. He said that there were a lot of really tricky things going on at his office and that he had to be careful who he trusted," she added.

Filby looked pointedly at St. Scot.

"Who found the body?" St. Scot asked, wanting to change the subject.

"Well, it was poor Helen, God bless her. After dinner, after I left, Bill went out to his workshop, you know, like he always does. That man can make a stuffed animal look positively alive…or at least he could," she said.

She wiped a tear from her eye and took a breath.

"What time was that?" asked Filby.

"This morning, she found him," she answered.

"No, I meant what time did Bill go out to his workshop?" Filby asked again.

"Oh, I guess I left around nine-thirty and so he went out after that…" she said. "When I left, Bill said he was going out to do some work," she added.

"When was the body found, did you say?" asked St. Scot. It seemed strange to talk about Bill Borgenson as a body.

"I don't know that I should be telling this, after the police already took my statement and all, but, well, when Helen woke up this morning, Bill weren't there," she said. "Not that it was unusual for Bill to stay out in his shop 'till late, but Helen said there weren't any sign he'd been in yet. The poor dear went out to check and found Bill spread out on the workshop floor with his head in a puddle of blood and his hand still gripping his gun. She called the police, then me, and then a bit later she called Barbara. The police have been working in the barn ever since," she said, lapsing into silence.

With nothing else to do, Filby drove St. Scot back to pick up his car. There was no conversation between them on the short drive.

As St. Scot got out of the Suburban, Filby said gruffly, "See you."

Borgenson had been the second in command at the magazine. It was always assumed he would be the next in line whenever Filby decided to retire. Borgenson never seemed to be in a hurry for that to happen. Indeed, he never seemed to be in a hurry for anything to happen. He had worked as an accountant for one of the industry's big players for a long time and then had moved quietly to automotive journalism. His specialty was historic essays on the great cars and racing drivers of the past. Quiet and studious, he seemed the exact opposite of the swashbuckling image most automotive journalists wanted the world to have of their profession. Everyone liked Borgenson, and his organizational skills and management abilities balanced Filby's extravagance and emotional outbursts. He was the detail man to Filby's view of the big picture. More than a few of his peers had wondered quietly how he would stand up to the pressure of filling Terrance Filby's enormous shoes. Now they would never find out.

The phone was ringing when St. Scot got back to the firehouse. He caught it just before the machine picked up. It was Blinsky.

"Where have you been?" he demanded. "I told you I was going to call you this morning," he added accusingly.

St. Scot looked at the phone and tried to remain calm. He didn't say anything.

"Well, it doesn't matter," Blinsky continued. "Listen, I'm going to go to Africa in your place. You need to stay at the office and get everything under control there and it's important for people to know that I'm in charge, so I am going to go on the Volkswagen trip instead of you. I've already called and told them."

With everything that had happened in the past twenty-four hours, St. Scot had completely forgotten he was supposed to fly to Morocco the next day. Volkswagen was putting the finishing touches on a new type of sport utility vehicle and already its Public Relations machine was cranking up to hype the vehicle. The trip was for background material, ostensibly to show how the company did its hot weather desert testing in North Africa. The plan was to fly to Newark and pick up a Royal Maroc flight to Casablanca. From there, a chartered propeller aircraft would fly a dozen journalists to a location several hundred miles into the Sahara where Volkswagen test engineers did their annual hot weather testing. The trip was really another boondoggle. The journalists would be wined and dined and treated like sheiks. Volkswagen wouldn't allow the journalists to write anything about the new vehicle, but they would be able to write about the hot weather tests. And the company's Public Relations department would get the reaction of several influential top editors to its new vehicle, to help sell an even bigger launch budget to its top management. St. Scot had never been to Morocco before and had been looking forward to the trip.

"Do you think that's a good idea, Ivan?" asked St Scot. "The people at the office really do need to meet you in order to start building a team around you," he added.

Blinsky's response cut him short. "I am a leader not a manager! It's your job to build the team, it's my job to lead the team and tell them where to go."

St. Scot thought about telling Blinsky where he could go. Instead, he said, "Bill Borgenson killed himself last night. The office will be in turmoil. Don't you think it would be a good place for you to show that you are in charge?"

Blinsky paused for a second on the other end of the line. St. Scot could almost hear him weighing the options.

"What do you mean by killed himself?"

"Shot himself in the head. He's dead."

"What do the police say?"

"I don't know. Suicide, I guess..."

"No," Blinsky said finally. "I am going on your trip, you stay here and hold down the fort. I'll be back next Friday. Goodbye." With that, Blinsky hung up the telephone and St. Scot was left listening to an empty line.

St. Scot sighed, hung up the phone and went about his usual Saturday errands. Having been gone for the week, his mail was several inches deep. Ali had sorted it into three neat stacks which she then placed on a small table near the mail slot in what passed for a front door. Allison Chalmers lived in an apartment building a block away. She was a highly mature nineteen year-old who lived with her mother and stepfather, and was the mother of a toddler named Ronald. Allison was bright and personable and, even with her unexpected motherhood, had worked hard to finish high school and was now considering college. St. Scot paid her weekly to come into the firehouse and sort his mail and water his plants. He was pretty sure she had a crush on him, since sometimes he would catch her looking at him with a steady gaze that made him uneasy. Acting upon the adoration of a teenage girl was something many better men had been unable to resist, but St. Scot was holding his ground by shutting down any possible romance.

He noticed that Ali had also sorted through his packages and put some fresh wildflowers in a vase on the table. He caught himself smiling, frowned suddenly and looked at the stack of boxes. He had an arrangement with the parcel delivery companies that they would deliver packages through a special one-way door set into the wall next to one of the big firehouse doors. There were several boxes, the majority of them press materials from car companies and a few with car parts and tools. Most car companies had gone to CD-ROM for their press kits and some were even using the internet exclusively. A few still liked to back everything up with bulky notebooks filled with technical specifications and product photographs of the company's lineup of next year's car models. St. Scot sometimes liked having a hard copy of press materials in his hands but, with all the information also going straight to the magazine office, he couldn't understand why companies would waste their money sending him additional copies at home. It was probably in some forlorn hope that he would be so captivated by the prose created by a Public Relations flack that he would spend his evenings reading car company press kits. Sadly, that was sometimes exactly what he did. Once again he realized that he really did need to get a life. Setting aside the packages of press materials, he noticed with satisfaction that the new metal-working hammer he had purchased over the internet had arrived. *Thank God for online purchasing.*

St. Scot cranked up his PowerMac and signed on to download his e-mail. He usually traveled with a laptop computer and was fairly diligent about checking his e-mail when he was on the road. He hadn't checked it since the desert shoot, however, so there was a big stack of incoming messages in his in-box. He quickly deleted the solicitations to make millions while working at home and the offers to increase his size and girth. *How did so many internet spammers get his e-mail address?*

Scanning through the list of remaining messages he saw that most were either press information updates from car companies or mail from one of the three, old car on-line hobby groups that he belonged to. One by one, he deleted those, too. His day had been pretty depressing and he wasn't in the mood to talk about the merits of cadmium plating over zinc plating on the bolts holding the rear axle onto a Stutz. Maybe another day, but not today. He was so busy deleting mail without opening it that he almost canceled an e-mail sent from WIMBORG@newtime.com. He was sliding his mouse over to the delete icon when it struck him that it was a message from William Borgenson, recently number two at the magazine and, even more recently, deceased.

CHAPTER 6

S t. Scot opened the e-mail and immediately looked at the time it had been sent. Ten-forty-two on Friday night. St. Scot was pretty sure he remembered the old lady had said that Bill had gone to his workshop sometime around ten. He shuddered involuntarily. *Would this be Borgenson's suicide note?*

```
Subj: Are you sure?
10:42 PM Eastern Daylight Time
Simon: You probably think I'm pretty pissed
at you right now. I know you think Ter-
ry is. Stabbed us in the back did you? Well,
that's what the world must think. Truth
is, there is money to be made here. A lot
of money. Let's get together tomorrow and
I'll tell you how. But if you say any-
thing to anyone, especially that idiot Blin-
sky, or Filby, or anyone at WPI then the
deal is off and you will end up being the
world's biggest fall guy. I'll call you tomor-
row and let you in on the clever little se-
cret, and how we're going to get rich.—Bill
```

St. Scot read the short note several times. It didn't sound like the note of someone who was going to kill himself. It didn't sound like the note of someone who was despondent over the loss of his job.

But the real question was what to do with it? It wasn't really a suicide note but it probably would interest the police. If Borgenson was planning on meeting with St. Scot, he couldn't very well do that if he were dead. So he must have thought he'd be around on Saturday morning, which meant his death wasn't something he had planned on. At least not at ten-forty-two last evening.

St. Scott did what he always did when he had a problem. He picked up the phone and called Terrance Filby.

"What do you want now?" Filby demanded.

"Listen Terry," St. Scot started. "I don't know what's going on, but something isn't right."

Filby interrupted, "There's a lot that isn't right, starting with you!"

St. Scot felt his anger rise. "Stop it Terry! Let me tell you something. I got an e-mail from Bill. He wrote it last night and I just opened it."

Filby interrupted again. "From Bill? Last night? What e-mail? What do you mean last night?" Filby's voice had an edge to it.

St. Scot repeated, "I just opened an e-mail that Bill sent to me last night, apparently just before he died."

Filby was very quiet for several seconds.

St. Scot spoke again. "Terry, Bill didn't sound like someone who was going to kill himself. He said he wanted to meet with me today about something that would make us a bunch of money. And he implied you knew something about it."

There was another long pause on the other end of the phone. Then Filby finally replied, "You really didn't know Bill all that well, did you? Listen Simon, he could be moody. I'm talking about really big mood swings. One minute he was on top of the world and the next was all gloom and doom. I think he probably sent you that e-mail and then suddenly got despondent and decided to do something else, something drastic. You had to know him to understand that was what he was like. Trust me."

St. Scot listened to Filby's careful and calm explanation. It was delivered so precisely that, for an instant, he had the impression that Filby had practiced it before.

"Maybe, but I have a problem. What do I do with the e-mail? Should I call the police and give it to them? Terry, my God, what if Bill was murdered?"

Filby rushed back at him. "Murdered! Don't be insane, Simon! Bill was an angry and disappointed man whose job you helped eliminate. Do whatever you want with the e-mail note. Take it to the police if you want to, just don't try and save your own conscience by suggesting Bill's death isn't directly related to the underhanded things you've been doing. Goodbye Simon!"

St. Scot sat for a long time looking into space. It didn't make any sense. Why wouldn't Filby talk with him and listen? Filby had always been a firebrand and highly emotional. But he was also smart. He'd drop the bluster and listen if he thought you had a point to make. But that wasn't the Terrance Filby he'd met with this morning or just spoken with on the phone. It was almost as if he was frightened of something. St. Scot glanced at his watch. It was already mid-afternoon and too much was happening. He needed to think everything through and the only way he knew to do that was by working on his cars. He pulled on his heavy leather shop apron, grabbed the package with the new metal-working hammer and walked to a corner of the firehouse garage. Just walking in made him feel good. Working on his cars would make him feel even better.

St. Scot loved the curves that Italian craftsmen created in the aluminum bodies of cars like Ferraris and Maseratis during the hand-built coachwork era in the fifties. Working with a few hammers and a couple of shot bags, they had rendered some of the most beautiful automotive artworks ever seen. Years earlier, St. Scot had written a feature story about some of the hotrod metal formers who had worked in California during the forties and fifties; men who could start with a few flat sheets of aluminum and build fuel and oil tanks or even whole Indianapolis racing cars with a few, well-placed hammer blows. The technique had always fascinated St. Scot and even before he'd ever thought of becoming a journalist he'd taken a night course in metal shaping at the local junior college. Since then, he'd worked at the craft and had devoted a small corner of his firehouse to practice his metalworking. His first attempts had been miserable, but the more he practiced the better he became and, lately, his skills had been steadily improving. He'd even done another story just so he could spend a few more days at the feet of the old men who still knew how to hammer metal into shapes. He realized he would never be an artisan at their level of skill, but he could produce workmanlike objects and could accurately re-create the curvatures for his friends who needed cycle fenders or oil catch tanks for their pre-War racers or motorcycles. He'd even made a few parts for several of Filby's cars before the collection had gotten too big and Filby hired Mort Welsh to take over. It was a great stress reliever and St. Scot found he could spend hours at the craft.

Taking a sheet of aluminum from his stock he carefully laid out the patterns he would need to cut. He had saved a pattern for nearly every piece of work he'd done. He usually started out with cardboard shapes and then, when he was happy with the result, would transfer them onto a sheet of pressboard. He'd cut out these now permanent patterns and store them in a sectioned bin in a corner of the fire station.

When he'd started out as a metalworker he used tin shears, just like they did in the old days. More recently, he'd purchased an air powered nibbler that cut more quickly and smoothly, with less pain to his hands. With the pieces now cut, he lit his acetylene torch and adjusted it to a sooty flame. He gently heated the aluminum pieces until they were covered in black soot, then set them aside and let them cool to an annealed state that would allow the aluminum to be easily formed.

St. Scot's thoughts shifted to everything that had been going on in the last few days. *Filby hated him and blamed him for Borgenson's death. Or did he? There was something about Filby's reaction on the phone, and the e-mail note. It made no sense. And what had Borgenson meant about being the world's biggest fall guy?*

St. Scot selected one of the aluminum pieces and cleaned the soot from it.

It'd almost sounded as though Borgenson had expected that he and Filby would be fired, that he knew that they'd be fired. How could that be?

St. Scot placed the flat piece of aluminum on the shot bag and began hitting it with his new wooden mallet. The center began to sink inward as the edges rolled upward. Soon the

rough shape of a fender appeared from the flat piece he'd started with.

*The biggest question was what did Blinsky have to do with it
all? Borgenson had told him not to talk with Blinsky. What could
that mean?*

Grabbing the roughly formed aluminum fender he placed it
on his large English wheel. This was a device that had one very
large and one very small roller that are pressed together with
a screw wheel operated with the foot. St. Scot set the initial
gap and began pushing his fender back and forth through the
two rolls. From time to time he'd kick the thickness adjuster
with his foot to pinch the rollers closer together and thin the
metal he was working on. Very soon, all of the hammer marks
were rolled out as the curve of the fender was refined. St. Scot
paused to compare the fender to one he'd made two weeks
earlier. Within a relatively short time the two fenders looked
identical. He found a hammer and tiny punch among the tools
on his workbench and inscribed three almost imperceptible
marks along the inside edge of the fender.

By the time St. Scot left his shop, daylight was gone and
it was well into dark. He skipped dinner and slipped into
bed. He still didn't have a clue about what he was going to do
about the e-mail, or about what was going on in general, but it
felt good to have done something that was both creative and
physically demanding. He fell into a dreamless sleep.

Sunday morning, with sunlight streaming through his windows he awoke to the sound of the telephone.

"Hello," he managed to croak out in a sleepy voice.

"Mr. St. Scot? This is detective Linda Jameson from the Sixty-Fourth Street station house…" The woman's voice was very businesslike.

"Yes, detective," he managed in a slightly more intelligible voice, sitting up now.

"Mr. St. Scot, I'm sorry for calling you on a Sunday morning," the woman began, sounding not the least bit sorry. "I wondered if you might be available to answer a few questions," she added.

"Questions? What kind of questions?" St. Scot asked, feeling somewhat alarmed. *Now what?*

"We'd like to ask you some questions regarding Mr. Borgenson. Would this afternoon work for you?"

Borgenson?

"Yes. Would one o'clock be okay?"

"Certainly. Fine. We'll see you then."

CHAPTER 7

After breakfast, St. Scot went to his office and attended to some things in preparation for the coming week and then, promptly at 1 p.m., he rolled up to the police department's downtown office in the new Lexus. He had dressed casually in khakis and a button-down shirt with tiny vertical blue and white stripes and a dark blue blazer with no tie. On his feet he had a pair of Sperry deck shoes. He was wearing the uniform of a successful businessman on his day off and he felt like he pulled it off pretty well.

The parking lot was mostly deserted and St. Scot found a visitor's spot near the large glass doors of the modern brick building. He identified himself to the front desk sergeant and was told to wait for the detective.

Detective Linda Jameson came out of her office and walked toward him. She was tall, maybe as much as six feet. Her straight dark hair was cut very short and for an instant St. Scot thought of the Olympic skater Dorothy Hamill. Like most adolescent boys in 1976, he'd had a crush on the champion skater. Jameson had that same kind of face. She looked to be in her mid-thirties and was dressed in the same uniform of careful casualness that St. Scot was trying to achieve: she wore khakis, a nice medium blue blouse and sensible shoes. Her clothes said this was a Sunday and the only reason she was in her office was because she was working on something important. Obviously they were reading from the same sartorial page.

She held out her hand and greeted him with a slight frown. St. Scot's eyes were drawn to hers. They were a light shade of green. *Oh great fall in love with a police detective...*

Jameson led him back to her office and sat down behind a large desk that was overflowing with papers and files. Her computer was running a screen saver program that showed a different racing scene from the fifties every twenty seconds. He recognized it as the same screensaver he had on his computer, created by a legendary female journalist from New Mexico who had actually taken the photographs of the famous cars when she herself was racing in Europe during that golden age. On the credenza behind her desk, Detective Jameson had three small model cars. One was an Austin Healey, carefully detailed to look like the car driven by female European rally legend Pat Moss. Next to it was a light blue Type 35 Bugatti racing car from the thirties, and the third model car was a small open roadster painted a moldy green. The lines were distinctive and St. Scot, who prided himself on knowing nearly every racing sports car from the postwar era, searched his memory in vain for the car's nameplate. St. Scot looked up to see the police detective looking at him.

"I am the detective in charge of the investigation into the death of William Borgenson," she began. "We are questioning anyone who might be able to provide us with information about this case. You understand that it is your right to have an attorney present and that you are waiving that right?"

"Yes, I understand," St. Scot said.

The detective looked through some papers on her desk and began to read aloud. "A single gunshot wound to the head. Small twenty-two caliber revolver. Didn't make much noise. We figure time of death sometime between 10 p.m. and midnight. We should have the coroner's report later." She stopped reading and looked directly at St. Scot. "How well did you know Mr. Borgenson?"

St. Scot reached into his blazer pocket and pulled out a sheet of paper he had printed that morning from his computer. Borgenson's e-mail. He handed the sheet to the detective. She read the e-mail slowly. He liked the way she looked as she read, the slight frown on her lips as she concentrated on the page. He looked at her fingers. No rings.

"I assume you're saying this e-mail came to you from Mr. Borgenson on the night he died?" she said, looking St. Scot squarely in the eye.

St. Scot replied, "Yes, I believe so. I opened that e-mail on Saturday afternoon and I wondered why a man who was going to commit suicide would be arranging a meeting for the next morning."

Jameson looked at him over the top of the page. She started to say something and then hesitated. "Have you told anyone else about this message?"

St. Scot thought of Filby's strange reaction to his phone call. "Just Terrance Filby," he said.

"And when was that?" she inquired.

"Right after I discovered it on my computer," he answered.

"Why did you call Mr. Filby?"

"He's my oldest friend and my mentor. I thought he might be able to help me figure out what to do with Bill's note."

"And what did he suggest?"

"He wasn't much help. He's still pretty sore about getting fired from his job at the magazine."

"The magazine Mr. Borgenson also worked at, is that right?"

"Yes," St. Scot replied.

Detective Jameson looked at him for a few seconds and then put the e-mail aside. "I'll keep this if you don't mind," she said. "Now, did you know Borgenson well?" she asked again.

St. Scot hesitated. "I thought I did. I worked with him for a dozen years and we always got along well. He wasn't a really outgoing person, but then neither am I. It was always assumed he would eventually be the boss at the magazine."

Jameson looked at her note pad. "Yes, there were some big changes at your magazine this week. I have already spoken with Mr. Filby and he stated that you were undermining both himself and Borgenson. That you were—as he said—in cahoots with the new owners. Is that true?"

St. Scot suddenly felt very tired. "No, it's not true. I know Terry thinks that's what's going on, but it just isn't that way. Look, I was out west all week on a story and when I got back I found Terry and Bill had been fired and that Ivan Blinsky had taken their place. I had nothing to do with any of that and I was just happy to still have a job."

Jameson looked at her notes. "Yes, Mr. Blinsky. Would you know his whereabouts?"

St. Scot smiled. "He's heading at this very minute for Morocco on a trip to the desert that I was supposed to take."

Jameson looked puzzled. "A trip to the desert? Why?" she asked.

"It's a press introduction for a new Volkswagen sport utility vehicle. I was supposed to go but Blinsky stole the trip away from me yesterday morning, deciding it was more important for him to go," St. Scot explained.

"I see," she said. "When did you see Borgenson last?" she asked.

"Last Monday, just before I left for the western trip," he replied.

"Did he give you any indication then that there might be something he wanted to talk with you about?" she asked.

"No, nothing," he answered. "It was just routine work talk."

"Can you tell me where you were on Friday evening?"

"I flew into the airport in the late afternoon, drove home and then returned to the Hilton at the Airport for a meeting with Ivan Blinsky. Then I drove back home and went to bed."

The detective looked up at him. "Was anybody else at that meeting?" she asked.

"Yes," answered St. Scot. "Winston Marshfield, Roland Beeson and several people I didn't know. All of them work for WPI, the new owners of the magazine."

The detective nodded her head as she wrote in her notebook. "And at what time did you return home?" she asked.

St. Scot shrugged and said "I guess I got home sometime after eight."

She nodded. "You didn't go out anytime after that?"

"No, I was beat from the trip and everything that had happened and just wanted to go to bed."

"I see. Well, Mr. St. Scot, I assume I can reach you at the number I called this morning if I have any other questions?" she said rising from behind her desk.

He had wanted to ask her about the screen saver and the sports car models behind her desk, but he hadn't found the moment.

"Look," he said hesitating, "I'm going to lunch nearby, just for a sandwich. Would you care to join me?"

Detective Jameson looked at him with a level gaze and answered "No, I don't think that would be appropriate."

Shut down.

St. Scot left the police station and went to a bistro up the street. He sat at a table near the door and ordered a grilled Portobello mushroom sandwich with waffle cut fries. It was warming up outside so he ordered a lemonade and downed half of it as soon as it arrived. He suddenly felt very hungry. The mushroom sandwich was good: a large Portobello marinated in an olive oil and balsamic vinegar mix and then grilled over an open flame. A piece of Swiss cheese was melted over the mushroom which was then placed on two slabs of toasted sourdough bread and covered with sautéed onions and smeared with a bit of Dijon mustard. The fries were crispy and St. Scot ordered some barbecue sauce to dip them into. He ate quickly, but enjoyed every bite. After another lemonade, he paid the bill and headed out to run some errands and get ready for what would face him the next morning at the magazine. He could only assume it would be another stressful day.

CHAPTER 8

Under Terrance Filby, working at the magazine had been a happy experience. Although the workload was always huge, the pace frantic and Filby prone to emotional outbursts, everyone had a good time. Unlike many of the competing magazines, turnover was low and headhunters had trouble getting people to even talk to them, let alone leave. Most of the staffers, from the young members to the well-established writers like St. Scot, were there for one reason: the chance to work with the legendary Filby. If you were good enough to cut it working for Terrance Filby, you were good enough to cut it anywhere.

St. Scot arrived at the office a little after eight the next morning. He knew that nobody would be there. The staff tended to filter in around ten, but made up for it by staying late most evenings. Filby never cared what time anyone arrived or left, as long as the work was done to his impeccable standards. The office itself was one of the perks of the job. It had once been a three-story machine manufacturing works, built in 1933. It was made from brick and wood and steel and still had the overhead power shafts running across its ceilings. The inside was huge and open. Filby had exquisitely renovated it at a cost that made even Bob and Zelda Fisher turn pale. He'd left much of the exterior brickwork exposed in the public areas and the oak beams that supported the front and bay doors were polished to a luster. When they'd bought the building, the district was rundown and it had seemed like a poor move. Now, a decade later, the area was one of the hottest markets in town and the building was worth ten times what they had into it, even with Filby's expensive renovation. Of course, now that WPI owned the building, the rumors were spreading that the mega-corporation would sell the historic landmark and move the magazine office to a strip mall in the suburbs. *Charming.*

St. Scot unlocked the front door and shut off the alarm system. The central part of the building was left open and its roughhewn wooden shop floor remained. Parked in the center were three of Filby's classic cars. Every month or so, Mort Welsh would rotate out one or two of the cars, bringing in others to replace them. Clustered around the cars were a few chairs and a low table. For most meetings, this was their conference area; surrounded by cars of the past. On the outer perimeter were offices for each of the writers and editors and a large bullpen with lots of natural light for the art department. The natural light wasn't such a critical commodity now that everything was done on powerful Macintosh computers, but it was a nice connection to the way magazines used to be put together with scissors and tape. Next to the art department was a large library filled with car books and back copies of car magazines from around the world. Even with the resources of the internet, this library was one of the magazine's biggest assets. Books from every era were housed in huge floor-to-ceiling bookshelves. If a magazine wanted accuracy, it was essential that it have these kinds of resources available. It was not uncommon for contributing writers to trust their research entirely to information that they'd downloaded from the internet. When the magazine's copy department began its laborious fact-checking process, the fallacy of trusting websites for information became clear. Speedy Gonzales' "SUPERCAR" website just wasn't a good enough source if you were writing a story for a respected magazine.

The walls of the library and, indeed, the walls of every part of the building were filled with posters and original automotive art from some of the best-known artists of that genre. Old car advertisements and posters announcing races and rallys filled the walls with splashes of color. Each was neatly framed and carefully hung to create exactly the right effect. In fact, sometimes the debate over art placement in the office would rage for hours, with Filby in the middle of the argument, usually in opposition to the opinions expressed by the art department. Like art departments everywhere, they felt like it was their role to be the final arbitrators of taste and style.

Behind a wall at the far end of the building was a full kitchen with a large conference room that doubled as a dining room. The kitchen was always in use and, in fact, several of the staff had arranged for a well-known local chef to give a month-long cooking class in the evenings, using the magazine's restaurant-grade equipment and facilities. A small storage room had been taken over as a wine cellar and staff people brought bottles from home to place in their own special sections of the wine racks. At the back of the building was a six-bay garage where special test cars and other projects were built and maintained away from prying eyes. To one side of the garage was a photo studio where it was possible to do the kind of studio shots car companies liked so much.

St. Scot went into his office, hung his blazer on an antique coat rack in the corner and sat down behind his desk. His office had the usual collections of model cars and decorative car parts that one would expect from a car guy who was working at an automotive magazine. He fired up his Macintosh and pulled up his e-mail. There were no messages. Next he checked his inter-office e-mail. There was a note from Filby sent last week reminding him about the Automotive Press luncheon on Wednesday. Filby was a heavy hitter in the community and had always made sure a few of his editors came to the press lunches to eat rubber chicken and hear the keynote speaker talk about some industry topic. St. Scot sent a quick e-mail to the organization's secretary to let her know that he would not be attending. As he looked at his inbox, what struck him almost immediately was that there were no inter-office notes addressed to him after Friday morning. *Hmm. Either the staff had been too stunned to send messages to one another or they believed he was a villain and had frozen him out of the loop.*

As St. Scot worked, he became aware of the office waking up around him. Lights were coming on as the staff arrived and settled into their offices to begin their day. He soon smelled the aroma of fresh coffee from the huge pot in the kitchen. He heard the low murmur of voices but unlike most mornings, nobody came to chat or came anywhere near his office. It was obvious they were avoiding him. His outside phone line began to ring and he waited for Maryanne to pick it up, before remembering she'd been fired on the previous Friday. He reached for the phone and punched a button, but the caller had already hung up. He took out a yellow legal pad and made a to-do list. At the top of the list he wrote "find a new receptionist." The next item was to find out when Borgenson's funeral was scheduled. He would close the office and give everyone the whole day off. He was pretty sure he had the power to do that.

He then decided to venture out to get some coffee. He had put it off as long as he could, but now he would have to face his staff. As he came out of his office he bumped straight into Meagan Timmons. The petite twenty-four-and-change assistant art director bounced off of him and looked frightened. He smiled at her and apologized for his clumsiness. She mumbled something and then scurried away, not wanting to look him in the eye. Meagan was usually a fountain of good cheer and bubbling with excitement.

St. Scot walked to the end of the offices and into the kitchen. Some of the staff members were near the coffee pot talking. As soon as he entered the room all talking stopped and everyone turned to look at him. The sudden silence was supremely awkward.

"Good morning everyone," St. Scot said with as much good cheer as he could muster.

One or two of the people at the other end of the room mumbled some sort of greeting. These were mid-western-ers after all. It wasn't in their genetic makeup to be rude to people. St. Scot walked to a shelf and picked out his favor-ite coffee mug. When the assembled crowd realized he in-tended to join them at the coffee pot they began to disperse, heading back to their offices. One of the last to go was Mark Summers. He looked St. Scot straight in the eye for a long second before turning without a word and walking away. Feeling hurt, St. Scot poured himself a cup of the French Roast blend coffee from the pot and returned to his office without seeing anyone else.

The morning passed slowly. St. Scot's phone didn't ring and nobody came into his office to see him. He had grown accustomed to being in the middle of things and was used to being interrupted constantly throughout the day; phone calls from Public Relations people and freelancers pitching stories added to the buzz that was his workday. This unusual silence made him edgy, but he didn't know what he should do. He worked on his Ferrari story, finished it and sent it to the art department for a layout. He sent an inter-office message to Summers asking him to find a receptionist from a temp agency right away. Summers hadn't sent him an answer and apparently someone from the staff was answering outside calls because the incoming phone line was no longer ringing non-stop. The only inter-office message he received that morning was a general one: Borgenson was being buried on Wednesday afternoon.

The rest of the day went by as slowly as the morning. St. Scot went to lunch by himself. He didn't know how to approach the people on his staff and was beginning to get angry. *How could they not trust him? How could they accuse him? They knew he would never do anything to hurt Terrance Filby or the magazine. What was wrong with everybody?* At the corner Italian place, he was so upset that he barely noticed that the pasta in pesto was overcooked and uninspired. In the afternoon, Mort Welsh stopped by with a two-car trailer to remove two of the three cars from the open, central part of the building. He then came back and retrieved the third. When St. Scot went to get more coffee later that afternoon, he noticed that the loss of the cars suddenly made the place seem big and empty. It no longer felt like the place he had worked in for so long. It was truly the end of an era.

By the time St. Scot left that evening, there was nobody else in the building. He grabbed his car keys from the board —the ones the magazine's motor gophers assigned, determining who would get what car each evening to ensure a fair rotation. With one glance, St. Scot saw that the gophers had exchanged his Lexus sedan for a Korean-built sport utility vehicle. Nobody on the staff had particularly liked the noisy little SUV and it sat neglected most of the time. Glancing at the board again he saw that his Lexus had gone to Meagan, and he had been relegated to the penalty box. Something needed to be done to address all of this nonsense, but he still hadn't figured out what exactly that would be. It was one thing to accuse him of treachery, but to make him drive a crummy car was an insult. Of one thing he was sure: the drab transportation matched his mood.

The next morning, St. Scot was back at his desk early. He checked his e-mail. There were only two messages, both from Becky Moore at Volkswagen's corporate communications office. Moore was in charge of the press trip to Morocco that Blinsky had commandeered from St. Scot. The first message was sent on Monday evening, which would have been early in the morning on Tuesday in Morocco:

```
Simon,
We haven't seen any sign of your
Mr. Blinsky. He was supposed to arrive in
Casablanca after flying first to Europe. My
people were waiting for him, but he never ar-
rived in Casablanca. I'm checking everything
```

I can from here and have turned the airlines
inside out, but can't seem to find him. Do
you know if he missed his first flight? We
delayed our charter flight to our desert en-
campment by two hours, hoping he would be
on the next flight. I'm worried what might
have happened to him and hope you can do
some checking on your end. Regards, Becky.

The second e-mail was posted early on Tuesday, late morning
in Morocco:

Mr. St. Scot,
Mr. Blinsky has arrived. He was late because
he was tired and decided to stay in Newark to
take a nap. When Mr. Blinsky arrived here in
Morocco and found none of us waiting for him,
he chartered an airplane to take him to our
desert camp. He was extremely rude to me when
he landed, wanting to know why he had been
left behind. He now also wants Volkswagen to
pay for his charter flight. His airplane charter was not authorized. He told the pilots that
he was a top executive at Volkswagen. He even
told them that they would be paid as soon as
they got him here. This is unacceptable behavior and I cannot imagine why you would have
sent Mr. Blinsky on our trip to represent your
magazine. In all of my years in this business, I can never remember a more disagree-
able person that I have had to deal with. In
the future, please do not send such arrogant and unqualified junior staff members on
our press trips, or the relationship between
your magazine and Volkswagen might be severely
strained. Also, can you please let me know how
you plan on covering the expense of Mr. Blinsky's charter flight? Regards, Becky Moore

St. Scot sat at his desk for a long time and tried to imagine
the ego of someone who would hire an airplane to make it to

a press conference because he wanted to take a nap. Finally he gave up and didn't send a reply to Becky Moore. What could he tell her? That Blinsky was an idiot? It was something she'd obviously already figured out for herself.

The rest of the day went as badly as the day before. St. Scot thought about calling a meeting to explain his side of things, but he was afraid of the reaction he might get. His relationship with the staff of the magazine had always been a genial one. He was older than many of them and they usually looked to him to be the guy in charge whenever anything went wrong. He knew it was fear that was holding him back, but he couldn't do anything about it. Maybe he really wasn't cut out to be the guy in charge. He cared too much about what people thought about him and wanted to be their friend.

So he tried a different tack and called a couple of his colleagues for advice. In each case, however, he was told by some receptionist that they were unavailable and that he should leave a number and they would call him back. These were guys he'd known for ten years or more, people he'd worked with and had helped out many times in the past by providing them with information or leads when their stories had run dry! They *owed* him, damn it! They'd never before been too busy to take his calls before, and now this?

It was pretty hard to consider people in the business as friends exactly, competition for jobs in the automotive journalist field was tough and there were always plenty of people waiting in the wings to take your place. Like any other profession, though, it had its fair share of charlatans and fakes. Still, if you had been around as long as he had, you knew who most of the good ones were and who the bad ones were. Most people had always considered him a good one, so what the hell was going on? How had he become persona non-grata over one short weekend?

The new receptionist Summers hired was young and bored, but at least the phones were being answered, although his own phone never rang once. He spent the day editing a very long story from one of the magazine's European contributors, a process he enjoyed, especially since the guy's first language wasn't English. Late in the afternoon, however, he was getting hungry and left the office, stopping at one of his favorite pizza places for a sausage calzone before going home. The thick crust of the Italian specialty was hot and chewy and the sausage and cheese filling was superb. He ate quickly, washing down his food with a Diet Dr. Pepper and headed home. At least his transportation today was better: the gophers had given him a new Ford F150 pickup truck.

When St. Scot arrived at his home, he noticed that his mail had been sorted and a single fresh flower was in the vase on the table. There were mostly bills and a couple of classic car magazines from Europe. St. Scot switched on his computer. The hard drive began to whir and then suddenly it started searching. After twenty seconds, everything went quiet. The screen was blank and none of the start-up procedures had appeared. Puzzled, St. Scot hit the reset button and waited. Nothing happened. He switched off the computer and checked all of the cables. Then he switched it on again. Still nothing. *The computer was dead.* He thanked his luck that he had transferred the Ferrari story onto his computer at work. He would lose a few things, but probably nothing that couldn't be reconstructed from his back-ups, and the last time he'd backed the hard drive was Monday, a week ago. And he was gone all last week, so the only things he would lose were his e-mails. Suddenly, St. Scot felt a chill. The only e-mail he had saved was the one from Borgenson, whose funeral he would attend tomorrow, and he'd given Detective Jameson a copy of that already. But now he had no way to prove where the page had come from. He quickly realized that he had to take the computer to the Macintosh repair center tomorrow, before Borgenson's funeral. He needed to know why this had happened. Something kept nagging at him about the loss of that e-mail file. *What had Bill Borgenson wanted to talk to him about?*

CHAPTER 9

The next day, St. Scot skipped going into the office and, instead, loaded his computer into the front seat of the truck.

The computer repair center was in a strip mall several towns over and St. Scot arrived just as the bearded proprietor, Jake Bergmann, pulled into the parking lot. They went into the shop together, each carrying a part of St. Scot's computer system. Although the inside of the place looked like vandals had recently ransacked it, St. Scot knew that it always looked this way.

Jake turned on the lights and moved behind the long, low counter at the back of the store. "So, what's the problem?" he asked.

"Well, it just sort of died. The hard drive doesn't want to start," answered St. Scot.

Jake scratched his head for a bit. "Sounds like its been infected with a virus," he stated decisively. "We've been seeing a lot of that lately…I'll have a look before the end of the day."

"Any chance I can have it back today?" asked St. Scot.

Jake shot him a withering glance. "Doubtful, dude! I'm not even sure what I'll be able to save if it's been hit with a destructive virus."

As he was leaving the shop, St. Scot glanced at his watch. It was too early to go to Borgensen's funeral and he didn't want to go back home. So he did what he did best. He drove out of town, into the countryside, and let his mind wander. As he drove, his eyes scoped out the areas behind barns and storage sheds for any sign of a classic car that might be rusting away in the shadows. The days of finding a Ferrari in a barn, left by a son who had gone to war and would never return, were over. This old urban legend had been told and retold so many times it was now accepted as part of car lore. Most of the truly great finds had already been made, but every once in a while he heard about something rare and unusual being dragged out of a field or from an old barn. In the last couple of years, two significant racing Jaguars and an important Shelby Cobra racer had been discovered. Covered with dust and with mouse-eaten upholstery, such barn-find cars had become the rage on the international auction scene, sometimes bringing more than a fully restored version of the car would realize. The argument was that cars were only original once and after you restored them they could never be original again. Apparently the rust was considered charming. Anyway, all St. Scot ever saw were rusting Chevrolet Citations and Chrysler K-cars from the 1980s and those cars had never been charming.

The parking lot outside of the funeral home looked like the display at an international auto show: Porsches, Corvettes, Range Rovers, BMWs and Mercedes-Benz sports cars and sedans. New cars and trucks were everywhere—press cars supplied to automotive editors who had come to pay their last respects to William Borgenson, one of their own.

As St. Scot pulled into the parking lot he saw a knot of his colleagues from another magazine entering the building. He parked the truck in the crowded lot and walked to the entrance. He was dressed in a somber dark suit with a white shirt and a subdued tie. Inside, small groups of people were standing and talking. Several of them looked up when he walked in and then went silent. Nobody greeted him and he felt the tension in the room rise dramatically. He was definitely alone. Finding his way to a seat in the middle rows of chairs, he was aware of his colleagues (*hell some of them were supposed to be his friends!*) carefully filling in the seats as far away from him as possible. *This was getting ridiculous!*

The service was short yet poignant. Terrance Filby said a few things about his old pal Bill Borgenson and few had dry eyes after that. Helen sat with Barbara Filby and St. Scot recognized the neighbor who had been at the house. No mention was made of how Borgenson had died and twenty minutes after it started, it was over, and the crowd quickly left for the procession to the cemetery. St. Scot held back and watched Terry help Helen and Barbara into a stretch limousine that pulled out to follow the hearse. He suddenly decided he didn't want to be a part of the parade of this year's newest vehicles and, instead, headed for the office. He figured that Borgenson, being dead, wouldn't mind too much if he missed seeing them plant him into the ground.

The office was empty, except for the new receptionist. She was reading a movie fan magazine and barely looked up when he arrived. St. Scot picked up his only message and went to his office. It was from Detective Jameson, asking him to call her. He made the call and heard her voice on the phone. She was as brusque as she had been in her office.

"Mr. St. Scot. Thank you for returning my call," she said. "I have spoken again with Mr. Filby and he mentioned that you and Mr. Borgenson had worked on several research projects for him, outside of your work at the magazine?"

"Um, yes, that's true." St. Scot was surprised that Filby had mentioned that to the cops.

"He said that you and Mr. Borgenson had a bit of a falling out over this work and that it had soured your friendship?"

St. Scot was stunned. "Terry said that?" he stammered. "No, that's not true! Bill and I got along fine, I just got too busy to work on those projects anymore and Bill took them over."

Why would Terry say these things?

"I see. Okay, well thank you Mr. St. Scot. We'll be in touch if we have any more questions. Oh, and Mr. St. Scot, please keep me informed if you are planning on leaving the state for any reason."

He booted up his computer and checked his e-mail, but there were no new messages. *How could that be?* He was always complaining about the number of e-mails he received and now there were none. Trying to quell his rising anger, he pulled up a story that had been submitted by one of his columnists and began editing it, hoping it would take his mind off of the stress of this other business. It was a good column, filled with reminisces of a simpler time when a dad could actually share the experience of working on a car with his son. In twenty years, would anyone ever reminisce about playing video games on computers with their dads? He sighed.

It was a topic St. Scot had written about before. Nobody could really work on a modern car anymore, at least not in a home garage. Cars had become better than they'd ever been in the past: faster, safer, more comfortable and infinitely more reliable. Microprocessors and computers had taken over nearly every system, from engine management and automatic transmission control to opening and closing the electric windows and tuning in the radio stations. Cars no longer had components like carburetors and distributors that the average shade-tree mechanic could understand and work on; they hadn't been equipped with such archaic devices for more than a decade. Instead, professional mechanics now needed computers to communicate with a customer's car to find out what part was ailing. Not that all this technology was bad, he mused. The requirements of meeting government regulations for exhaust emissions and fuel economy had actually forced automakers to develop solutions that had the added benefits of performance and reliability. St. Scot had no problem with useful technical marvels. It was the next series of innovations, which often seemed to be technology for the sake of technology; that had him concerned.

He had already driven prototype cars that had a pair of joysticks instead of a steering wheel and brake and gas pedals. Similarly, he had driven cars with radar control that could detect a car ahead, and automatically apply the brakes to avoid a collision. He had ridden in cars that automatically steered themselves, based upon cameras that detected the edges of the roadway. Driver optional. While some might argue that such features were safety innovations, St. Scot felt uneasy about anything that removed the already ham-fisted driver from the equation. Of course with cell phones, faxes, personal computers, e-mail, voice recognition systems, navigation systems, refrigerators, drink coolers and microwave ovens all integrated into the cockpit of cars of the near future, he doubted how much time drivers would have to spare for their driving anyway.

An hour and a half went by and St. Scot figured people would be getting back to their offices after the funeral. His own staff had the rest of the day off, but he tried to think of someone who could tell him what he had done to become such a pariah. Elizabeth Meyers came to mind. A few weeks earlier, she had been hot on his trail to come and join her company. Hadn't she said "New information has come to light," just before rescinding her offer? Maybe she could tell him what the hell was going on. He left his office and went out to the pickup truck in the parking lot. He needed to see Elizabeth at once.

CHAPTER 10

Elizabeth Meyers was a bigger-than-life legend in the automotive industry. She and her late husband had started their communications company directly out of college in the 1970s as a way to protest against the automobile and all it stood for. They became closely involved with critics like Ralph Nader and Joan Claybrook and had quickly become a thorn in the side of industry leaders. Their barbed press releases on the inability of the industry to solve problems and their scathing criticism of efforts on safety and the environment became textbook examples of how to manage a smear campaign in the public eye. It didn't hurt the company one bit that Meyers was one of the most beautiful women that anyone had ever seen. Her flashing green eyes, long auburn hair and luminous skin were made for television and she became a popular guest on national talk shows. Her husband was equally handsome, closely resembling the Robert Redford journalist character in "All the President's Men." Most people figured that Elizabeth was the brains behind the operation but nobody could deny they were both strikingly beautiful and enormously powerful. Then, one day, her husband was coming back from a meeting in Washington when he had a sudden and completely unexpected heart attack and died. Elizabeth Meyers was left alone with the business, her memories and a one-and-a-half million-dollar life insurance settlement. Meyers Communications immediately closed its doors and its glamorous owner disappeared.

A year later, in a new building in a fashionable suburb, a new Meyers Communications arose. Gone was the commitment to safety, the environment and left-wing causes. Meyers Communications quickly grabbed some big-name automotive supplier corporations as its clients and set about doing corporate public relations with a vengeance. Her staff was all young and clean cut and what they lacked in experience and wisdom they made up for with hard work and a fear of their iron-willed leader. The women who worked for Meyers were all beautiful and the men all exceedingly handsome. Jealous rumors outside the company abounded about how she kept herself entertained with such a staff, but nobody could argue with success as Meyers Communications, again, became a major force in the auto industry.

For a brief time a few years ago St. Scot had provided Meyers with a pleasant diversion. Neither had planned it and, from St. Scot's view, it had been all too brief. He had enjoyed being seen with such a major player as his colleagues shook their heads in amazement when they showed up together at press dinners and corporate functions. Everyone figured that she was way out of his league. Even St. Scot knew that she was way out of his league. And, as much as he enjoyed the attention and envy of those around him, and as incredible as they had been together physically, they rarely had much beyond business to talk about. Maybe she got tired of slumming because shortly after St. Scot had returned from a two-week new car introduction in Europe, he found that their fling was over.

When St. Scot arrived at Meyers Communications, he was led into Elizabeth's office by an executive secretary who could have easily found work as a male model. The office was enormous, with floor to ceiling windows on two sides. In addition to the desk, she had a credenza that was open to reveal a laptop computer. In one corner of the room was an oval-shaped conference table with a few chairs surrounding it. The overall impression was one of light and order and, above all, success. Meyers rose from her large Swedish Modern desk and came forward to meet him. She too was dressed for success, wearing a cream colored silk blouse under a tailored chocolate-brown silk blazer over a tan skirt that ended just above her knee. Her dark red hair fell loosely around her shoulders and she was wearing a pair of steel-rimmed reading glasses. As much as he tried to prevent it, even after all of the time that had passed, and even though he had promised himself he wouldn't let it, St. Scot's heart jumped. And then it jumped again.

Elizabeth's manner toward St. Scot was cold and formal, however. No heart jumping for her, it appeared.

"Simon, I don't know why you have come and I don't care. I don't want to see you," she said.

"Elizabeth, we need to just talk for a minute. I need your help."

With a heavy sigh, indicating evident reluctance, she led him to a chair one side of the desk and, turning gracefully, moved back and took a seat on the far side.

St. Scot thought for a second. This was going to be tricky. "Listen, Elizabeth, we've known each other for a long time and been through a lot together, and you know I've always respected you." He paused. No response. He pressed on. "Look, I'm going to lay my cards on the table. Something is going on and I don't know what it is. I thought it was a reaction over Terry and Bill and the situation at the magazine, but now I think there must be more, and I was hoping… hell, Elizabeth, I'm asking you outright, what are people saying about me?"

St. Scot had tried not to sound desperate, but in the end the words had just come tumbling out.

There was a long continued silence. Finally, Meyers spoke. "Simon, we are speaking completely off the record. If any of this ever gets back to me, my lawyers will tear you apart. Do you understand?" She paused. He nodded. She continued. "Simon, someone with great credibility and power within this business came to me last Friday with certain information. Information about you." Meyers paused again and St. Scot pushed through it.

"Well?" he asked, more angrily than he'd intended.

"The information convinced me that you are dirty. That you are involved in some very shady business deals with some very dishonest people and that you have been embezzling money from your magazine."

St. Scot shook his head. "What? That's insane!" he protested. "Who is saying such things?"

"Let's just say they have proof, and if they choose to prosecute, you would be found guilty." She paused again. "And then there's the matter of you and Bill Borgenson," she went on. "They're saying you murdered him in cold blood. Simon, I know you. Or at least I thought I did. I just don't know what to believe…" Meyers' voice trailed off.

St. Scot was speechless. Finally he asked quietly, "Who is doing this to me Elizabeth? Who came to you with these lies?" For an instant St. Scot thought Meyers might tell him, but then he heard her voice close that door.

"Simon, you need to get help. Professional help. Find a lawyer. Turn yourself in. Make a confession. Maybe they'll go easy on you," she said.

He started to say something when Meyers said sadly, "Simon, I had always hoped we might be able to work together. And maybe more. I always liked you and your writing, and I wanted to find a place for you here. I'm just sorry that it can never be. Now I'm asking you to leave." She stood and walked over to the door, which she opened and held for him as he walked out past her.

He felt numb. No wonder he was being treated like he had the plague. If those were the rumors that were being spread among his peers, just what was getting to the police?

Their romance hadn't lasted long, but they had remained friends—until now. She had been the one person in the world who he thought he could turn to, and now that one person thought he was a crook and a murderer.

Chapter 11

The low slung sports car hugged the curve, its narrow tires screaming in protest as its wire wheels flashed brightly in the sunlight. St. Scot worked the four-spoke steering wheel, shuffling it back and forth as the car traced a graceful arc through the corner. He was dressed in his brown leather jacket and was wearing a leather flying helmet and a pair of old aviator-style goggles. The wind whipped around the pair of minimal Brooklands racing aero windscreens that replaced the car's usual full-width windshield. It was a 1951 Jaguar XK120 roadster and St. Scot was wringing all of the performance out of it on a private test track, so that evocative photographs could be taken of the old Jaguar at full song. Lap after lap he hurled the car past the photographer in lurid slides that would give the art director what he wanted, illustrating the glory of this old British racing-green warrior. For a brief time, for St. Scot nothing else existed except the old sports car and its tenuous grip on the pavement.

St. Scot had driven to the track for the photo shoot that morning. For some reason (that he didn't want to question) the gophers had stopped punishing him with pickup trucks and sport utility vehicles and had given him a bright red

Porsche Boxster S to drive and he'd enjoyed the 45-mile trip through the countryside. It'd been a cool morning and he'd arrived at the track with the top down and his jacket collar pulled up against the wind. The owner of the Jaguar was a jolly, white-haired retiree who had once run a major plastics manufacturing company. He had owned the Jaguar from new and had raced it in the 1950s, before putting it away so that he could build a family and his company. Now, with his kids running the company, he had time to have the Jaguar completely restored and ran the car in vintage races all around the country. St. Scot had met him several months earlier when he'd written the story about the restoration and they'd been planning the track photography session for several months, but bad weather and mechanical problems kept intervening. So far it had been a great morning and, best of all, the elderly gentleman knew nothing of St. Scot's problems so he was as friendly as could be.

Now, strapped into the Jaguar's soft leather seats, he was able to forget, for a brief time, the weight of the problems he was facing. The view of the louvered hood over the racing windscreens, the low rumble of the XK straight six-cylinder engine and the whine of the Moss gearbox mixed with stray whiffs of hot oil and racing gasoline melded into a sublime feast for the senses. It was always fun to drive someone else's car around a racetrack.

It had been less than twenty-four hours since Elizabeth Meyers had hit him with the news that all of his associates and co-workers believed him to be a thief and a murderer. At least now he could understand why everyone was treating him with such suspicion and contempt, but it brought him no closer to knowing who would be spreading such insidious rumors. He had tried desperately to think of who could be behind the accusations, but he was no nearer a solution now than he had been when Meyers had given him the information.

He'd heard the rumors about automotive journalists who had been caught taking kickbacks from advertisers in exchange for good car reviews. There were even stories of press cars being delivered with suitcases full of cash in the trunk with no questions asked when the car was returned empty. But those things had happened years earlier. Nobody could possibly believe they could happen today—not that everyone in the business were saints or angels, there was plenty of opportunity for dishonesty, but not for Simon St. Scot. *I'm one of the good guys!*

Simon St. Scot had been working as an automotive journalist for fifteen years. He'd started as a freelance writer shortly after graduating from college with a master's degree in journalism. His college sweetheart had become his wife and they had lived mostly on her salary as a nurse. Nurses made a lot more money than beginning writers did. Even so, there'd been a few lean years until he had found a home with Terrance Filby at the Fisher's magazine. Filby had seen something in a freelance piece St. Scot had done for another magazine and had asked him to join the big time. The travel had been almost continuous and the strain too much for his wife, who left him and found a nice stable doctor to marry. St. Scot had come into the journalism game just as most of the true old-timers were retiring or dying off, and he'd listen to the stories that they told of all-week drunks, hot and cold running hookers and epic automobile collisions, with the wide-eyed wonder of a Boy Scout sitting around a campfire. In the old days, if a car magazine wasn't wrecking two or three test cars a month they were looked on as wimps: press cars in swimming pools, banzai cross-country drives and childish behavior ruled in those days before political correctness and deadly sexually transmitted diseases existed.

Although much tamer today, it was still an imperfect system. The car companies paid his way for what, thirty trips a year? Well, that wasn't quite accurate either because at least half the time he would combine trips together. The car companies had gotten pretty good at communicating with each other and it made better sense for them. If BMW was flying a group over to Munich for a technical program, then Jaguar might take some part of the group to England for a drive in Wales after the BMW trip ended. That way, BMW would only have to pay business class airfare one way across the Atlantic and Jaguar would pick up the costs for the flight back. (Automotive journalists always flew business class when going overseas.) St. Scot would typically go to Europe six or seven times a year and Japan or another part of Asia at least once every two years. He made it a point to stay over for an extra day whenever he went overseas, just so he could do some sightseeing on his own, and a lot of times the companies would pick up the tab for his extra night in a hotel. He would never actually ask them to do this but, more often than not, when he went to check out he would find his room was already paid for. Except for a few of the newspapers that had strict rules about who paid for what, all of this was standard practice. None of it would raise an eye amongst his colleagues. The embezzlement sins he was being accused of now, however, must be on a different level altogether.

After the photo shoot, on his drive back from the racetrack, he broke one of his own rules against using the cell phone and called Jake Bergman, the computer geek.

"Dude," Bergman said when he heard it was St. Scot, "your computer is toast. Some sort of virus. The operating system is history and almost everything on your hard drive has been corrupted. It's fried, man."

St. Scot dreaded asking the next question. "Is there anything you can do to save any of my files? I had some important stuff on it…"

"Well, I know a few tricks that might work to get back some of it. But man, whatever got your computer was pretty aggressive. Much worse than any I've seen before."

Stacked against the attacks on his character that some unknown person was making, the computer infection seemed like little more than a stuffy nose. St. Scot asked Jake to do what he could as he rang off.

Friday morning, St. Scot slept uncharacteristically late. He finally rolled out of bed and made it to the office by ten-thirty. People avoided him and only the receptionist greeted him, albeit in a subdued way. Apparently she had also been tipped off about his supposed indiscretions. Again, he had almost no e-mail. St. Scot tried to think of anyone who could help figure out who was out to get him. But who? He had always liked the image of a loner, sort of the Steve McQueen type who got by fine with a minimum of acquaintances and few friends. Well, now this attitude was working against him. He couldn't think of anyone he could call to help him make sense out of this. He felt lost and alone. Some Steve McQueen.

When St. Scot arrived back from lunch, there was a message from Blinsky that he would be arriving back from Morocco on the three-thirty flight from Newark that afternoon. There was no indication that St. Scot was supposed to pick him up or arrange transportation or hotels, but he figured he may as well go to the airport and meet him as he got off the flight. At least Blinsky was still talking to him.

The Northwest Airlines flight from Newark arrived exactly on time. Blinsky was the third person off the airplane. He was wearing a fez. He looked absurd.

"You look like shit," was the first thing Blinsky said as he walked up to St. Scot.

"Well, it's been a tough week," said St. Scot.

Blinsky peered at him and said, "Oh come on. How hard can it be to run the magazine for a week? But don't worry, I'm here now and everything will go more smoothly."

St. Scot started to say something and then thought better of it. Getting angry with his new boss first thing wouldn't be a good start.

They went to pick up Blinsky's two large suitcases at the baggage claim area and St. Scot paced with disapproval while they waited. Automotive journalists learn early to travel light, with only one or two carry-on bags. They don't trust the airlines with their luggage and they hate waiting to see if they will win the baggage claim lottery. But here was Blinsky with two huge suitcases and he seemed perfectly happy to wait for them as the baggage carousel went around and around. St. Scot stopped pacing and tried deep breathing instead, thinking that maybe he should take up yoga.

The bags finally arrived. St. Scot grabbed one and headed for the exit. Blinsky took the other one and followed. As they strode through the parking lot and out to the car, St. Scot turned to Blinsky and asked "where are you staying?"

Blinsky looked uncomfortable for a second and said, "Well, Simon, I don't have a house yet and although I adore hotels I thought maybe you would let me stay with you?"

St. Scot tried not to let his shock show on his face. With everything that was happening to him, he did not want to have a houseguest and especially a houseguest who promised to be as big a pain in the ass as Blinsky would undoubtedly be, and especially a houseguest who was his new boss. The silence stretched on between them before St. Scot finally said, "Sure, Ivan. I'd be glad to have you stay with me while you figure out where you'll live."

Blinsky looked satisfied. "Great!"

They arrived at the firehouse in the Porsche. One of the suitcases hadn't fit in the limited trunk space so Blinsky had ridden with it on his lap. As they pulled up to the big double doors, Blinsky's eyes widened.

"You live here?" he asked incredulously.

"Yes, for six years now," replied St. Scot. Simon got out of the car, undid the locks and then drove the car into one of the empty bays. He closed the door behind him, helped Blinsky remove the suitcase from the trunk and then carried it up into the living area of his firehouse home. St. Scot had two spare bedrooms in the living area, although one of them was piled high with boxes and magazines. The other was reasonably clear of such debris and St. Scot installed Blinsky in this room. St. Scot found a spare key for Blinsky and showed him how to work the security system.

For dinner they walked three blocks to an Asian fusion restaurant. Blinsky had finally ditched the fez, having replaced it with a white Panama hat. St. Scot, who was fond of fedoras, wondered idly how Blinsky had managed to transport the Panama in his suitcase, all the way from Africa, without crushing it.

St. Scot had barbecued prawns on a bed of rice with lemon grass. The seafood had been splashed with teriyaki sauce and the flavor mix with the lemon was quite pleasant. Blinsky order Pad Thai and proclaimed the dish to be just a bit too spicy. They drank Japanese Kirin beer with their food. Making use of the unexpected time with Blinsky, St. Scot tried to get a handle on his new boss.

"I got an e-mail from Becky Moore at Volkswagen while you were away," St. Scot began, looking for any reaction from his dinner companion. Blinsky didn't even pause in his eating.

"She seemed quite upset about how you arrived at their little camp in the desert," he went on.

Blinsky slowly stopped eating and put his fork down beside his plate. He looked straight at St. Scot for a half minute before finally sighing. "She doesn't know what she's talking about. I mean, the woman is completely incompetent. How could they leave me stranded in Casablanca with no way to find them? I thought my solution was ingenious," Blinsky said, looking rather proud of himself.

St. Scot ignored Blinsky's arrogance and continued. "I also got a strange e-mail from Bill Borgenson on the night that he died," he said, while calmly taking another sip of beer.

This time there was a reaction. Blinsky who had started eating again stopped the travel of his fork from his plate to his mouth. "What kind of e-mail?" he asked, slowly letting the food slip off of his fork and back onto the plate.

"Well, it was strange," St. Scot replied. "He said he wanted to meet with me about something important. What was strange is that it didn't sound like a note from someone who was about to kill himself." St. Scot looked Blinsky straight in the eyes while he said this.

Blinsky looked uneasy. "Who did you show this note to? I mean, did you show it to anyone?" Blinsky asked.

"Yes, I talked to Terry about it on Saturday and then showed it to a police detective on Sunday," St. Scot said.

"The police! Why did you call the police?" Blinsky exploded.

"Well, I didn't call them, they called me and, it seemed like it would be a good idea to go see them when they asked me to," St. Scot stated with a slight edge to his voice.

"Do you have a copy of this note?" Blinsky pressed, clearly agitated.

"Well, that's the problem," St. Scot answered slowly, more pointedly now. "My computer crashed earlier this week and I didn't have another hard copy of the note, and the detective kept the one I showed her..." St. Scot trailed off, watching Blinsky's reaction.

Blinsky shook his head. "I just wish you hadn't gone to the police with this," he mumbled.

Seeing that Blinsky was obviously upset and thinking he maybe knew more than St. Scot had suspected, he went on. "Ivan, I am having some personal problems," Blinsky looked at him across the table carefully. "Somebody, I don't know who, but somebody is saying bad things about me," St. Scot said.

Suddenly, Blinsky regained his composure and all of his former agitation disappeared completely. "Simon, you need to do something about this paranoia of yours."

St. Scot interrupted, his voice rising, "Ivan, they're saying I'm stealing money, that maybe I had something to do with Bill's death, that I'm dirty and am about to be arrested! The staff at the magazine hates me for it and I'm being frozen out of the rest of the business."

St. Scot was now leaning across the table at Blinsky, face to face.

Blinsky slowly buttered a piece of sourdough bread before saying, "Yes, I know that Simon. I know all about you."

Chapter 12

For several long minutes Blinsky continued to eat his Asian food and sip his Japanese beer. St. Scot sat back down, trying to slow his heart rate, and said nothing.

Finally, Blinsky spoke. "WPI, actually, I mean it was Winston Marshfield who told me, when they offered me this job, that you have a history of taking money and sort of a general dishonesty; that you and Borgenson had some sort of scheme planned and that you had a violent streak that could get you into trouble. Apparently it has..."

St. Scot started to protest but Blinsky cut him off. "Don't bother to deny it. Look at how you live and all of those great cars. You can't get those on a journalist's salary. Besides, I've seen the stuff that Marshfield has that proves everything," Blinsky said confidently.

St. Scot sat dumbstruck. *What the hell could they have on him?*

"But don't worry about any of that, Simon. It's okay. Really it is. I, and, of course, WPI, can use a guy like you. That's why they had to get rid of Filby and Borgenson and brought me in. They figured you and I could work together and make the magazine even more successful than it ever was under Filby and those other owners, the Fishers. I mean, someone like you who is willing to break a few rules now and then can be very useful in business." Blinsky looked smug and proud of himself.

St. Scot felt sick. "I quit," he said slowly and with a level tone.

Blinsky smiled at him sadly. "Don't be stupid. You can't quit. If you tried to, Marshfield would be able to have you indicted for all kinds of embezzlement and fraud. Probably murder, too. He has all the proof he needs. I wouldn't worry so much if I were you. For now, just keep doing what you have been doing and occasionally write a review that favors whoever it needs to favor. Just like you've been doing all along."

St. Scot felt his anger rise. His voice began to crack as he said, "Let me make one thing absolutely clear, you piece of shit. I have never ever written anything that was done to satisfy an advertiser." St. Scot's voice broke and he choked on his words.

Blinsky just looked at him sadly. "I saw what Marshfield has on you, Simon. Don't try and act all holier-than-thou. I have seen the proof. It's okay and you don't have to worry. Damn it, Simon, just play along. Nothing has to change. You'll see. You and I are going far in this business."

St. Scot got up from the table and walked straight out of the restaurant. He needed air. He needed help. He needed something. He needed to be away from that smug asshole Blinsky. At least he finally knew what was happening, and it made him sick. He always figured he was one of the good guys, doing what was right and reporting on the transgressions of others. Okay, so it wasn't Woodward and Bernstein and what he really did was write for an automotive enthusiast's entertainment magazine, but damn it, he had always sort of felt like what he did was important. He helped people make good choices when it came time to buy a new car, he told stories that made people want to become car guys, he lived out other people's fantasies for them. He loved that life. How had it been made to seem so suddenly rotten and sordid?

St. Scot got to the door of the firehouse and looked behind him. Blinsky was a half a block back and in no hurry to catch up. St. Scot unlocked the side door and left it open so that Blinsky could get in. He went straight to his bedroom and closed the door. He didn't want to see Blinsky or anyone else. What he wanted was to get drunk and the bottle of brandy on his dresser helped him do just that. *How could they do this to him?* The first shot of brandy provided no answers. Neither did the next three. The rest he didn't remember.

In the morning, St. Scot heard a car pull up in front of the firehouse. Bleary-eyed, he looked out of his bedroom window. It was a taxi. The driver sounded the horn and the noise pierced St. Scot's hung-over skull like a needle. A few minutes later Blinsky, struggling mightily with the two huge suitcases, stumbled out of the door to the waiting taxi. The driver loaded both the bags into the car and Blinsky, hesitating for a moment, looked back at the fire station before getting into the cab. Seconds later the taxi pulled away from the curb and drove off.

St. Scot flopped back on his bed. He didn't normally drink much and his hangover from the brandy was acute. He pulled the covers over his head and slept until midday. When he did get up, he showered and had a bowl of cereal before lying down again for another nap. Finally, in the late afternoon, hunger drove him from his bed and he ordered a pizza for delivery. The place had slow service and by the time his extra-cheese-with-mushrooms-and-thick-crust arrived he was starved. He wolfed down four pieces and barely noticed it. By the fifth piece, he was beginning to think more clearly. What he needed to figure out was what they could possibly have on him. He needed a plan of action.

First, he tried to think of all of the stories he had written in the past three or four years. He thought mostly about the fluff pieces he had written. Everyone in the business occasionally wrote a fluff piece. It was usually a non-story about some new product that had recently been advertised in the pages of the magazine. There was nothing in a fluff piece that was untrue, but there was also no real scrutiny of the product or harsh comparisons against any competitors. It was easy to justify as a way to tell readers about new products or introduce them to a new manufacturer. Fluff pieces really made the advertising guys happy.

St. Scot well knew that every successful commercial magazine has an ongoing battle between the church, represented by editorial, and the state, whose role is played by advertising. There is, in theory, a strict separation between church and state. Further, the old school says that people buy and read a magazine because of its editorial content. But the truth is that with all of the subscription deals available, readers don't really pay for the costs of writing and running a magazine. That's what advertising does. The system breaks down, however, when the publisher acts as a go-between, with a foot in each camp. When that happens, editors scream bloody murder that they are being corrupted by advertising's filthy lucre and the advertising department wails that their filthy lucre is the only thing keeping the whole enterprise afloat. Both are right, of course.

St. Scot couldn't think of any outlandish claims he had made in any of the half a dozen fluff pieces he had written in the past few years. He then tried to think of what cover stories he had recently been involved with.

Cover stories in a major enthusiast magazine were a car company's fondest desire. All of the press trips, the exotic locations and pampered treatments were really in search of the elusive cover. When you figured a monthly magazine only did twelve covers each year, the chances of getting your car out front seemed pretty slim. The goal here was to beat the competition in newsstand sales. The magazine cover had to break through the clutter of the newsstand and grab people who stopped by an airport magazine store or their local Barnes & Noble and make them buy. For a long time St. Scot bought into the idea that the car on the cover would make a difference. Finally, though, he began to realize that the phase of the moon or the current Dow numbers had at least as much to do with what sold on a newsstand. But what St. Scot thought didn't matter. Guys in charge, guys like Filby, kept hammering home the importance of the cover. The ad guys and their clients figured that covers were pure gold so, during the course of any given year, heavy pressure was placed on the editorial staff to put cars on the covers that would be further supported by lots of advertising dollars.

St. Scot couldn't see anything that would raise a flag and cause his world to come crashing down around him in that regard. It was fairly ordinary practice in the life of an editor of an automotive magazine. No, he felt quite certain, after thinking about everything, that what they had on him wasn't something he had done or written. But that really meant a decidedly more sinister alternative: the damning evidence that was ruining his life and that was being accepted as truth had been specifically fabricated to achieve his downfall and obedience. The question was why?

On Monday afternoon, St. Scot was supposed to fly to Colorado Springs. Cadillac was presenting a new version of its latest personal luxury coupe to the press; this was a long lead, attended by mostly the top magazines and a few of the better-known automotive freelancers. His mind kept going back to the one consistent theme, and that was that it seemed that the key to the whole mess was Winston Marshfield. After what Blinsky told him the other night, it seemed that flying to New York and finding out what exactly Marshfield had on him was the only plan that made any sense. If the airline schedules would cooperate, he could make it to New York Sunday afternoon, meet with Marshfield on Monday morning and still make it to Colorado Springs by late Monday afternoon. It was worth trying. He had to find out what was going on. St. Scot picked up the telephone and booked the flight to New York.

CHAPTER 13

St. Scot flew into New York Sunday evening and took a taxi to a trendy, private hotel where he'd stayed before, not far from WPI's headquarters. The Royalton's foyer and attending bar were well-known hangouts for the rich and famous of New York; they served a martini that was the talk of the town.

Entering the chrome and glass lobby, he walked to the check-in desk and signed the guest registry, leaving his credit card imprint for incidentals. A bellhop carried his one bag to the elevator and they made their way in silence to the 5th floor. They arrived and walked down the dimly lit hall to Rm. 510. The bellhop opened the door for St. Scot, placed his bag inside the door, received his tip and left. St. Scot walked into the room and looked around. Each time he stayed here he chose a different room, each decorated in its own way. This room was filled with art deco light fixtures and a rigid-looking but surprisingly comfortable bed. He was tired, but hungry, so he went back downstairs and found a nearby deli that was still open. He had hot pastrami on onion rye with a knife-full of hot mustard and washed it down with a Genesee beer. Nothing like going native when in New York.

It was raining the next morning when he left the hotel. He trudged the three blocks through the wet city streets, wearing an overcoat and a fedora as if it were 1957. He couldn't help but feel just a bit like Cary Grant, this time in the Hitchcock movie *North by Northwest*. Men just don't wear hats very much any more. Some say it is the fault of President John F. Kennedy, who went to his inauguration hatless and forever changed men's fashions. If so, in St. Scot's eye, the thirty-fifth President of the United States had a lot to answer for.

WPI's offices were in a mid-town Manhattan skyscraper. The company's sheer size and its variety of business interests meant that several floors were dedicated to each division. St. Scot entered the glass and steel building and walked up to the guard at the reception desk in the building's lobby. He quickly flashed his employee identification badge from the magazine and brusquely asked to be directed to Winston Marshfield's office. The guard told him that the office was on the 23rd floor and that he should take one of the elevators on the right. St. Scot thanked him with a nod and walked purposefully to the elevators. As he rode upward, the elevator music played quietly in the background. It felt like a long ride up. His palms were sweaty and his overcoat suddenly seemed too warm. He knew what he was there for, but he dreaded meeting with Marshfield and wished he were back home and his life was normal again.

Finally, the doors opened into a large reception area done in an attractive if somewhat austere dove gray. Expensive artwork graced the walls and St. Scot reflected that, if they were genuine, the sale of just the paintings he could see would result in enough cash to pay for the cost of running the magazine for more than five years. He dropped his bag next to the elevator.

The receptionist sitting at a desk at one end of the room asked if she could help him. Just as he was about to speak, another elevator door behind him slid open and Winston Marshfield walked into the reception area.

Marshfield was dressed in his outer coat, dark gray and streaked with rain. No hat. St. Scot turned to face him and was struck by the fact that Marshfield was a good three inches shorter than he. St. Scot had always thought of him as being taller. Marshfield looked at St. Scot without recognizing him for an instant before it suddenly dawned on him who was standing directly before him, blocking his way into the inner sanctum of offices behind the receptionist's desk.

"What are you doing here?" Winston Marshfield said with hostility in his voice.

St. Scot stood a bit taller and tried to look menacing. "We need to talk about what you are trying to do to me and to my magazine!" St. Scot said louder and more forcefully than he had intended.

"Your magazine?" roared Marshfield. "There is nothing about that magazine that is yours and you're only still employed there because Ivan Blinsky says that he needs you, though I can't imagine why..." Marshfield said. "As for what's being done to you, you are getting what you deserve. You writer-types disgust me. You think that the whole magazine business revolves around you. Well, it doesn't. You are just a tool. One that is worn-out and no longer useful. It's time you discovered that. Ivan told you to just play along and keep your mouth shut, but you're just too stupid to get the message aren't you?

Well, maybe from now on we just won't be so subtle. Now get the hell out of my office before I call security!" With that Marshfield started to push past St. Scot.

St. Scot grabbed the man by the shoulder and spun him around, his right fist balled up in rage. He might have actually hit him, he certainly wanted to, but a glint of light against a small chromed revolver that had appeared in Marshfield's hand brought him up short. Marshfield smiled a wicked little smile that contorted his face as he pushed the revolver into St. Scot's ribs.

"Now, listen to me, Mr. St. Scot," he said venomously. "You will do what you are told to do and you will do it without talking to the police or Filby or anybody else. Do you understand?" In his present position with a gun stuck between his ribs, St. Scot felt it would be undiplomatic to disagree. "Now get out while you can still walk out!" Marshfield said, his cold blue eyes displaying intense hatred. The WPI executive then turned and walked into the hallway behind the reception desk, leaving St. Scot standing in front of the somewhat startled receptionist who quickly looked down and tried to appear absorbed in the papers that littered her desk. With as much dignity as he could muster, St. Scot turned and pressed the elevator button. Mercifully, an elevator car came quickly and he was soon in a taxi on his way back to the airport.

CHAPTER 14

S t. Scot arrived at the Colorado Springs airport later that afternoon and was met by a young woman from Cadillac's Public Relations agency. She was dressed in khakis and a red golf shirt and held a sign with Cadillac's corporate symbol on it. St. Scot was ushered into a Cadillac limousine and driven straight to the Broadmoor Hotel. He had stayed there before and appreciated its comfortable, old-world luxury. Cadillac had set up a special table in the lobby and the keys to his room were waiting.

His room was situated in the back part of the hotel, overlooking a part of the golf course and the walking trail. There was a welcoming fruit basket, a bottle of Colorado Creek sparkling mineral water and a note from Cadillac's Director of Public Relations inviting him to a cocktail reception that evening on the terrace, followed by dinner in the hotel restaurant. There was also a black Cadillac baseball cap, and a red Cadillac golf shirt. St. Scot reset his watch to the new time zone and stretched out on the bed to rest before the reception started. His encounter with Marshfield that morning had unnerved him. He had expected an argument and harsh words, not an outright threat of violence.

Maybe being here would help him work out what to do next. At least it got him away from the intense distrust of the people in his office and away from that asshole Blinsky. He shut his eyes and willed himself to turn his mind off, and slept.

The main topic of conversation at Cadillac's evening reception was golf. St. Scot didn't play but almost every car company executive in Detroit did, with an almost religious fervor. In fact, many times the venue for a new vehicle press launch was carefully selected to allow the car company executives a chance to play a few rounds at a prestigious course. Like racing drivers, golfers seemed to derive almost as much pleasure from talking about their narrow escapes and stellar achievements as they did actually doing the deeds.

About half the people in the room were dressed in the now familiar Cadillac red shirts. The uniform of the day also included a pair of khaki pants and loafers with tassels. Several of the top executives had thrown a blazer over the ensemble in an effort to show they were the ones in charge. *Why do men think this is a good look?* St. Scot wondered. To his mind, the outfit made most look like a vice-president of sales for a pipe and wrench company at a plumber's convention in Dubuque. St. Scot, on the other hand, had chosen a pair of olive trousers in light wool, a dark blue cotton shirt, red Hermes tie and black wool blazer. His shoes were black leather since this was an evening event.

There was an open bar at the far end of the dimly lit room and St. Scot ordered a Vodka Martini with two olives. After his trip to New York he felt like he deserved it. In the center of the room were large tables covered with food. St. Scot noted the requisite pile of three types of cheeses, the cut and sliced vegetables, the trays of miniature egg and spring rolls and the puff pastry rolled over tiny sausages. He noted with approval a huge pile of shrimp lying atop shaved ice. Some people judged a party by the brands of liqueur in the bar but, in truth, the shrimp were always the key. At a catered affair, each shrimp costs around three dollars. If a company wants to save money, it has tuxedo-clad servers carrying platters of shrimp around the room, discretely offering them one at a time to the guests. If a company has money to burn, the shrimp comes in great mounds and shoals of automotive journalists will surround the pile with three or four of the sea bugs on their plates. There were never any leftover shrimp at a reception when automotive writers were invited. Actually, there was almost never any leftover food after any automotive journalist feeding frenzy. St. Scot moseyed over to the shrimp and piled a half-dozen onto his plate. He had to keep his strength up, after all.

He looked around the room and recognized most of the faces. It was a mix of first and second-string journalists. Acquaintances in this group were plentiful, but friendships were hard to come by. Many of the journalists in the room lived within ten miles of St. Scot, yet the only time he ever saw them was on press trips halfway across the country or in far-flung parts of the world. It wasn't that anyone was particularly anti-social, they were simply busy. But it was also more than that. Writing, by its nature, is a fairly solitary thing and the profession seemed to draw in people who watched the world from the sidelines and reported upon it. This required a certain aloofness that also spilled over into a journalist's personal life;

those who found it too lonely could always find a guy from Public Relations to buy drinks for them at the bar.

St. Scot figured it was safe to assume that everyone in the room knew about his problems. This was a small community that dealt with gossip the way a drug addict deals with heroin: trading it for other juicy bits to get a high. Information is power and having more than someone else not only elevates your status, it can put you on the track of a story that nobody else has. It could even lead to a story resulting in a Pulitzer Prize. Okay, that was going a bit far, but the pressure to do better than anyone else was intense. A few journalists greeted St. Scot coolly, others ignored him completely. He was getting used to the routine. Everyone studiously avoided talking directly about Filby, Bill Borgenson or St. Scot's problems.

Several of the hovering Public Relations types were pulling Cadillac's executives from journalist to journalist, introducing them and letting them chat for a few minutes before pulling them to the next target. St. Scot had met many of Cadillac's brass on previous occasions and he was greeted warmly by the head of Marketing and Sales and by the company's middle-aged chief engineer. The talk was polite but superficial. It's hard to have a serious, in-depth conversation when you have a mouth full of shrimp.

Dinner was predictable. The appetizer was a vegetable tureen. The salad was mixed greens. Main course: prime rib, twice baked potatoes, green beans. The dessert was chocolate cake. The white and red wines were from California and cigars were offered after dinner with a selection of brandies and liqueurs. It was like a page taken from "What Corporate America Eats."

At dinner, St. Scot was seated next to Cadillac's chief engineer and one of the company's Public Relations flacks. Most of the evening the conversation centered on the engineer's 1932 Ford street rod project.

"We found an original flathead engine up in a barn in Canada, and got the frame and radiator from those guys in California," the engineer explained between mouthfuls. "I was going to go all retro, but decided I wanted modern radial tires, so of course that meant I needed better brakes and suspension, not to mention steering,"

St. Scot nodded and said, "I see."

"Oh I know what you're thinking," the engineer added. "You think I should have gone with a small block Chevy motor, aren't you? Well, I would have, but I did want to keep some parts original…"

What St. Scot couldn't figure out was why so many of Detroit's car company chiefs had suddenly fallen in love with hot rods. It was all the rage. If you were going to be considered a serious car guy in Detroit, you had to have a hot rod. The odd thing was, no matter what company they worked for, it was considered okay for them to build a Ford rod. In fact, it was important that it be a Ford, similar in every way to everyone else's Ford hot rod. *Bizarre.* It wasn't as though they ever took them to shows or drove them. Maybe, like golf, it was a guy thing that gave them something that would annoy their wives and that they could talk about at parties. The flack seated next to him meanwhile was cheerfully promising him a busy, exciting and fun-filled day at the racetrack. He winced at so much enthusiasm. As soon as he could, St. Scot left and headed up to his room.

St. Scot was up early the next morning and had breakfast in the main dining room. He munched his granola and yogurt with fruit while watching the herd of journalists graze on scrambled eggs, bacon, breakfast sausage, biscuits, white gravy, sugar-coated danish and buttered toast at the ubiquitous breakfast buffet. The calorie intake would have been appropriate for an expedition whose morning's goal was an overland march to the South Pole. This wasn't exactly what Cadillac had in mind for their day.

The program started with a bus ride from the Broadmoor to the racetrack. St. Scot sat by himself on the bus and read the local Colorado Springs newspaper. There was a story about a local schoolteacher whose life had been ruined when she won millions in the lottery, and another about the dangers of pesticides in non-organically grown rice. *Fascinating stuff.*

Pikes Peak International Raceway sits about twenty miles outside of Colorado Springs. It's a brand new racetrack dominated by a huge paved and banked one-mile oval track. It also has a token road racing circuit of 1.3 miles that uses part of the banked oval along with a portion of the infield. St. Scot could remember the old days when racetracks used to be grimy, disreputable places slightly below a pool hall in the scheme of public decency. That changed when huge amounts of corporate money were dumped into the sport to make it an alternate to traditional advertising. Coming to a racetrack to watch Jeff or Rusty or Dale drive their corporate-sponsored race cars became a respectable family activity and most racetracks are now efficient and squeaky clean. Pikes Peak Raceway is well-landscaped, everything is freshly painted and even the restrooms are *clean and friendly*. To St. Scot, it was a bit like visiting Disneyworld.

At the track, the group of twenty journalists was ushered into a conference room for a one-hour program about the new performance-version of the latest Cadillac coupe. Since it had been at least a half an hour since they had last eaten, almost everyone was relieved to see a stack of fresh danish and coffee at the back of the conference room. (Thank God there was more food!) This caused a fifteen-minute delay while everyone poured coffee and selected a gooey sugar-coated confection to bring to their seats. The program began with a five minute video with loud rock music and flashing images of improbably dressed young people living far richer and more fulfilled lives because they had chosen the *Mark of Excellence.*

Next, the marketing guys talked about wanting to attract younger buyers. This was not a surprise. Every marketing presentation that St. Scot had been to for the past five years had provided the startling news that the company in question was looking for younger buyers. The fact that these hypothetical "younger buyers" could never really afford a mid-or high-level luxury car seemed to escape the legions of automotive marketeers. The real truth was it was more fun to come up with marketing programs aimed at skateboarders and mountain bikers than it was to push tin at retirement homes and senior citizen centers.

The engineers were then given a few minutes to talk about the performance enhancements that the car had received; nothing earth-shaking, (certainly not compared to the news that the company wanted younger buyers) although the electronic suspension recalibrations caught St. Scot's eye. He began to formulate in his mind how he would write an extensive technology sidebar to the main story about Cadillac's ability to electronically tune the car's suspension. He made a mental note to pull aside the chief engineer at some point during the day for an interview.

Next on the program were several driving exercises using the new Cadillac. Outside, there was a row of new Cadillacs lined up for the journalists to use. St. Scot smiled to himself when he saw them, reminded of the tale that journalists told around the bar late at night. Back in the old days, a certain veteran journalist arrived late at a track event sponsored by Cadillac. The person in question was known for drinking prodigious amounts of alcohol and had done so for most of the previous night at Cadillac's expense. When he arrived at the racetrack the next day, he saw a long line of Cadillacs and, before anyone could stop him, jumped into the nearest one and roared out onto the racetrack. Lap after lap the auto writer hammered the car clumsily around the track. When he finally pulled into the pits the front tires were in shreds and the engine was boiling over. The journalist threw the keys at a Cadillac representative and went in search of food and beverage, leaving the Public Relations people to calm the irate caterer, whose two-year old Cadillac had just been the subject of the auto writer's abusive test drive. To top it off, the final story written by the journalist was full of praise for the new Cadillac model, even though he never actually drove one during his drunken weekend. *Ah, the good old days.*

Some of the driving exercises in-store were flat-out blasts around the road-course facilities or wet and dry road comparisons between the Cadillac and its several competitors. The racetrack was laid out in such a way to allow these activities to all take place at the same time. Cadillac had brought along Audi, BMW and Mercedes-Benz models for direct comparisons to its own cars and, although the comparison numbers generated at an event like this were meaningless, the fact that a company like Cadillac felt they belonged in such a distinguished group of automobiles was, in itself, significant.

St. Scot ran through the tests with a young Cadillac engineer in the passenger seat. He usually preferred to drive alone on these track tests, but he had met the engineer before and knew that he was an amateur racing driver on weekends. St. Scot was impressed by the work done by the industrious Cadillac engineers. The new car handled well, with none of the floaty imprecision of its predecessors. Ride comfort was sacrificed slightly, but was no worse than the sporty BMW. The car was especially good in the hard left-hander coming off the banking, and all of the electronic gizmos and stability systems helped keep the car in line as St. Scot buried his foot on the brakes. He was scrubbing off more than 60-mph for a corner from over 125-mph on the straight.

The young man sitting next to him was suitably impressed.

"I took the car out for some set-up laps yesterday," he said, "but I never got it much over 115 into that corner. I think you get onto the power coming onto the straight lots earlier than I do."

St. Scot took the Cadillac for another lap and talked his way through.

"See? I'm working a slightly earlier apex in the corner before the straight, knowing that the banking will catch me before my exit gets too wide." St. Scot enjoyed demonstrating his driving technique to his appreciative and captive audience. Lap after lap he held his braking as late as he dared, but still the Cadillac shed its speed without any drama.

"Good brakes," said St. Scot, as they rolled to a stop and got out.

Lunch came in the nick of time since the first symptoms of starvation were already evident in many of Cadillac's guests. Scurvy isn't pretty. After lunch St. Scot managed to corner the chief engineer for a three-quarters of an hour in-depth interview. By two in the afternoon, he was finished and ready to leave early, taking a specially arranged limousine to the airport to catch his flight to Houston. His red-shirted Cadillac host bade him farewell.

"You won't have time to get in any golfing?" he asked St. Scot.

"No, sorry, not this time," he answered, trying not to let his acute disappointment show.

CHAPTER 15

St. Scot drove his rental Buick into the driveway of the anonymous-looking industrial park. Wayne Robbins, sitting next to him in the small car, looked skeptical.

"This is where America's next world-class supercar is coming from?" he asked with more than his usual large measure of sarcasm.

St. Scot had arrived in Houston the previous evening after an uneventful flight from Colorado Springs. Robbins had arrived earlier and was already checked into his inexpensive hotel at the Hobbe International Airport. They had gotten together in the hotel bar for burgers and beers as they plotted their next day. St. Scot figured if they got an early start he could meet Bill Wilden, drive and photograph his new and super-secret American-made sports car, and be back on a plane heading home by late afternoon. That would give him a chance to plan how he was going to handle the magazine's editorial meeting the following day. It would be the first formal meeting between his new boss Blinsky and the magazine staff and he wanted to use it to diffuse the animosity that the staff felt towards him.

Although Robbins was based on the West Coast, the magazine used his photography skills quite often. He had apparently heard rumblings through the automotive media grapevine of St. Scot's problems, because, after a mountain of small talk, the photographer finally asked him, "So what the hell is going on with you?"

St. Scot looked at his old friend and sighed. "Wayne, I've been set up by Marshfield and Blinsky and I don't know who else at WPI. They have me in a tough spot, but I really can't figure out what it is that they want from me."

Robbins nodded his head sadly. "That makes more sense than what I heard. I heard you were stealing dough and selling out. Cool. I hope it works out for you, man."

St. Scot parked the rental Buick in front of one of the long steel warehouses. A small sign over the door said Wilden Industrial Design. He looked at Robbins and shrugged. "Let's go and meet the next Enzo Ferrari," he suggested.

The inside of the building didn't match its drab exterior. The carpets in the reception area were a rich Berber in a mocha brown and the large desk, behind which sat a pretty blonde receptionist, was mahogany. The walls were covered with a light cream-colored grass cloth and there wasn't a fluorescent light to be seen.

The woman seated at the desk smiled at them warmly and in a lovely and cultured British accent said, "You must be Mr. St. Scot and Mr. Robbins. Mr. Wilden will be happy to know you have arrived. I will let him know that you are here. Please help yourself to coffee."

Robbins found the cappuccino machine in the corner of the room and sent the apparatus into hissing fits as he made himself a large cup. St. Scot wandered around the reception area looking carefully at the artwork on the walls. Half of the tastefully framed paintings were automotive-related and St. Scot recognized several Bill Neale prints and a couple of Michael Turner originals. Looking around the room, two things were clear: this guy Wilden had good taste and he had the money to do something about it.

William Robert Wilden burst into the room looking like a stereotypical Texas oil tycoon. And actually, because he was a Texas oil tycoon, it was a look he could easily pull off. St. Scot was immediately reminded of J.R. Ewing, on the old *Dallas* television show. Billy Bob wore blue jeans, cowboy boots, a string tie and an improbably huge silver belt buckle. Wilden held out his hand and, with a winning smile, walked up to St. Scot and introduced himself.

"Simon St. Scot? I thought so! I recognized you from some pictures of you in your magazine. Damn fine! So glad you could make it, son. And you brought your photographer, too. Great. Just great. Come on back into my office and we can get started. Monica honey, hold all of my calls."

St. Scot and Robbins were ushered by Wilden through the door and into a hallway. On the right side, huge glass windows opened onto a very large and well-equipped workshop. St. Scot recognized several computer-controlled five-axis machines for complex metal work and a pair of large composite autoclaves used to make parts from lightweight aerospace carbon fiber material. Several white-coated workers were hovering around the machines. As they walked past an open doorway on the left St. Scot saw a dimly lit room with a series of computer-aided design workstations of the latest type. It was apparent Wilden only wanted the best of everything.

As they walked into Wilden's office at the end of the hall, St. Scot halfway expected to see a stuffed longhorn on the wall and a mechanical bull prominently in the center. It would have been in keeping with Wilden's demeanor. He was faintly disappointed when he discovered that he couldn't have been more wrong. Inside the office, in the center of the room, sat a mid-sixties, rear-engine Lotus Indianapolis racing car. St. Scot was drawn to it like a magnet. The car was scuffed and tired looking but, in its own way, noble and purposeful. Wilden beamed as St. Scot walked around the car admiringly.

"It's original, just as it came off the track," Wilden explained. "It was a backup car and was just run once or twice before being pushed aside to concentrate on the primary car."

Knowing Lotus history at Indianapolis, something about this story didn't ring true to St. Scot, but Wilden wouldn't be the first person who had purchased a fictitious history along with an old racing car and St. Scot wasn't in the mood to dispute his claims.

"It's a great conversation piece to keep in your office, Mr. Wilden," St. Scot said politely.

"Please, call me William," said the Texas oilman.

Really? William? Not Billy? Not Billy Bob? Not Tex? They moved away from the old racing warrior and over to Wilden's huge mahogany desk at the far end of the room.

As they took their seats, a sudden transformation occurred. Suddenly, Mr. Glad-hand Billy Bob Tex Wilden's demeanor changed completely. His face took on a serious note and his ah-shucks Texas accent disappeared.

"Gentlemen, let's dispense with the bullshit," he said in a flat mid-western voice. "I was born in Texas but grew up both here and in England, where I acquired a taste for racing and racing cars. I even raced a bit of Formula Two while there, but my parents didn't approve. They said it was too dangerous. Dad owned a pretty good number of the oil wells in Texas and his money talked."

St. Scot took out his notebook and began writing.

"We had a few Ferraris," Wilden continued, "and other exotics. Maseratis, a Lamborghini or two, stuff like that. My dad even had a Ford GT40 for a while, but sold it because it was too hot to drive here in Texas." Wilden closed his eyes and slowly shook his head at the thought. Finally he continued. "Like many other car guys in America, I always figured I could do a better job than the Europeans at building an all-American sports car. Carroll Shelby was from around here and did a pretty fair job, but he was really just interested in racing. Briggs Cunningham was another. He even got into trouble with the IRS because he was building too many racing cars and not enough street machines to be a real manufacturer. There have been others, including, most recently, that guy building the Panoz. But he is really a racer, too, or at least is mostly interested in racing cars. Well, all of those are pretty good success stories but none of them have built an American Ferrari and that's what I am aiming to do."

St. Scot looked at Wilden carefully. He was obviously rich, successful, well-educated and secure. St. Scot guessed him to be in his mid-forties, about the age of Enzo Ferrari when he started building his first sports cars. *Why would someone like that suddenly decide he needed to build a better mousetrap? Was there something in the psyche of men like this that made them desire to prove to the world that they could do the masters one better?* St. Scot had heard it all before and was pretty sure he knew what was coming next.

Wilden continued. "Of course, all of this takes three things. It takes a brilliant concept, and I think what I am going to show you fits that bill. It takes superb engineering, American engineering like the kind that took us to the moon." Wilden was getting wound up now and his showman's Texas accent was creeping back into his speech. "And, last of all, it takes the support of other Americans who believe in the dream." St. Scot knew for sure what was next and Wilden didn't disappoint him. "In a couple of months we will be going public with an IPO stock plan that should help us raise two-hundred-and-seventy million dollars to begin the production of our car. That's why I brought you here today. I want you to look at our car, I want you to drive it a bit and then I want you to spread the word that we are for real. This is going to be the biggest automotive story since Ford introduced his Model T, and I wanted your magazine to be the first to have it."

St. Scot had heard this song and dance before. The story never changed. Stock analysts would want publicity for Wilden's car before they recommended that anyone buy the stock during the initial public offering, a story about the car in a top automotive magazine would help make the idea of an American supercar legitimate, and the money that was raised would never be enough—of course.

Some amount of it would go to the actual engineering but more of it would line the pockets of the "money people" who were putting together the whole deal. St. Scot figured the chances of the car ever being sold were one in a hundred. He would end up being used by Wilden and the "money men", helping them make even more money. On the other hand, St. Scot also knew he was being just as disingenuous with his own agenda as Wilden was with his—the idea was that Robbins would take some very sexy photographs of whatever car Wilden had managed to cobble together, St. Scot would drive the prototype slowly around the premises (making sure that Robbins had a photograph of him doing so) and the story would probably be on the cover of the magazine with blazing headlines proclaiming "Exclusive First Drive! We Try America's New 220 MPH Supercar!" The cover would sell magazines and Wilden would get the publicity for his analysts. There was a strong competition among the magazines that kept guys like Wilden in the public spotlight while selling more and more magazines on the newsstands. It had happened before. It would happen again. There would always be a guy like William Wilden ready to use someone else's money to try and make his own dream come true.

Wilden continued in his fervor. "We, here at Wilden Industries, are really perfectly suited to build America's supercar. You see," he went on, "what we do is specialized machining and composite fabrication work for the U.S. government. It means we have the necessary knowledge to do some really high level engineering and the skills needed to build the things we design." There was a knock at the door and a bespectacled young man pushed the door open.

"Ah, Benjamin, I was just going to call you. These are the guys from the magazine, the ones who are writing about the Mysteria. Gentlemen, I'd like you to meet my chief designer, Benjamin Courtwright."

Courtwright nodded his head. "How do you do," he said with an English accent. "Mr. Wilden wanted me to answer any questions you might have about computer-aided design."

Robbins tried to stifle a yawn. St. Scot tried to think of something to ask.

"Um, well, okay. Tell me what sort of work station and software package you use." St. Scot feigned rapt attention as the British engineer spent five minutes describing in excruciating detail exactly which system he used and why. When he was finished, even Wilden looked bored.

"Okay Benjamin, why don't you take Mr. Robbins here out into the workshop and get some pictures of your computer setup?" said Wilden.

Robbins and Courtwright left and Wilden pulled his chair around to face St. Scot.

"You know, for what I am paying you guys in advertising fees that guy Filby said I should expect to get some pretty top drawer coverage," Wilden said suddenly.

Well, there it was. St. Scot thought about explaining to Wilden about church and state, but there was no point. A man like Wilden would never see the distinction. Still, he had to try.

"William, look. I'm not sure what Filby told you, but the editorial side of a magazine is different than the advertising side. When you buy ad space, you are doing just that, buying space on the page. But the editorial content of the magazine can't be bought. Our readers trust us to tell the truth and they wouldn't stand for it if our opinions were for sale."

Wilden looked confused. "Sure, sure, I know. But when you buy as many pages in as many of WPI's magazines as I've arranged to, well you have the right to expect special treatment."

"I'm hoping that your car and the work you've done here will stand on its own merits," said St. Scot charitably.

"That's all I'm saying," said Wilden, sounding even more confused.

The two men left the big office and went out onto the shop floor. As they passed through the shop they came to a door that led to a four-bay garage. Here were two swoopy sports cars, one a coupe and the other an open convertible. Their styling was atrocious, sort of a combination of a Pontiac Fiero and the Batmobile. St. Scot walked over to Robbins, who rolled his eyes. Wilden just beamed.

"These, gentlemen, are the first prototypes of the Wilden Mysteria," Wilden said with great enthusiasm.

"How am I supposed to make these pigs look good?" Robbins whispered to St. Scot.

St. Scot ignored him and stepped closer to peer at the engine visible in the car nearest him with its hood open. It was clearly a Ford modular V-8, the same one found in late-model Lincolns.

Wilden stepped up quickly and said, "That's just a mule engine for now. Eventually we'll design our own V-12 for the car. But we wanted to get our testing program underway and the modular V-8 seemed like it would be a good fit."

St. Scot asked, "Does your project have any official backing within Ford then?"

Wilden looked uncomfortable. "No, not really official, although they liked what they saw when they came by a few weeks ago," he said vaguely.

I'd wager not, thought St. Scot to himself.

Changing the subject, Wilden said, "I would like you to be the first person outside of the company to drive the car. We've arranged for the landing strip next to the complex to be free for your use. Shall we get started?"

Wilden pointed enthusiastically to the open roadster. St. Scot lowered himself into the cockpit and turned the key. The car started with a roar and settled down to a muffled idle. St. Scot drove the open car carefully out of the garage and along the industrial building to a row of hangars at one end of a paved airstrip. Inside the hangars were a couple of corporate jets and several smaller private aircraft. Robbins followed along, riding in the bed of a pickup truck that Wilden was driving. They needed to get some moving shots with St. Scot behind the wheel, but the stark industrial landscape wasn't very conducive to artistic photography. In reality, the crummy backgrounds wouldn't matter, since the images would eventually be manipulated on the computer anyway. The interior of the Mysteria was hard plastic and bare metal and since there was no provision for air conditioning, the hot sun beating down on St. Scot made him glad to be in the open car. When he reached the landing strip, St. Scot gunned the Ford engine and the car squirted ahead awkwardly. *Okay, he thought, in addition to being ugly, it also isn't very good.* St. Scot made several passes at moderate speed while Robbins shot roll after roll of film. St. Scot kept the creaking and clanking sports car prototype to less than 50 mph because at any higher speeds it shook terribly. Every little bump caused the chassis to corkscrew and lose composure. For St. Scot, driving this rolling abomination was a nightmare come true. Finally, having had enough, he drove it back to the garage. Wilden jumped out of the pickup and greeted him with great anticipation.

"Well?" he drawled. "What did you think? Did you like it? I know it needs a bit more development, but we are making progress each day. You should come back in a week or two and see the advancements we'll have made."

St. Scot nodded his head and made a few noncommittal comments. The car really was horrible, but he and Robbins had gotten what they needed for the exclusive cover story and Wilden would get his publicity to make his stock analysts happy. St. Scot was amazed at Wilden's absolute faith in this car. He was either an amateur con-man or he was absolutely clueless about car design and handling, or maybe he was so caught up in his own dream that he couldn't see reality. At any rate, the shoot was over and the article would be written. Time to go home. With a brief goodbye, St. Scot and Robbins were back in their rental car and headed toward the airport.

Ten minutes before boarding, St. Scot decided to check his phone messages. There were two messages from Blinsky wanting to know why he wasn't at work. *Had he forgotten that St. Scot would be out of town on assignment?* The last message was from Mark Summers. He sounded very upset. Blinsky had called a surprise editorial meeting and had made it clear that he wanted changes. Big changes. Story ideas would now be run through the advertising department first to make sure they made financial sense before wasting any editorial space in the magazine. Summers said that the staff was outraged, but Blinsky had made it clear that it wasn't open for discussion. Summers had ended with a plea to St. Scot to talk to "your friend Blinsky" and make him see how wrong he was. St. Scot shook his head sadly. What could he do? He didn't know what was going on anymore than the staff did.

After takeoff, St. Scot broke out his laptop and wrote the Cadillac piece. The comments from the chief engineer had been exactly what St. Scot needed to make the story sound like it had come from an insider. The company had come a long way and St. Scot figured they deserved credit for building such a competent sports coupe. He was thankful that he was able to lose himself in his writing. For an hour and a half he didn't think about the trouble he was in or what might be waiting for him when he got back home.

CHAPTER 16

When he arrived home, St. Scot found that Ali had carefully placed an international air express package on top of his other mail. The return address was The Honorable Vladimir Portunoff, Middlesex, England. *Great, thought St. Scot, another Russian.*

St. Scot knew Vladimir Portunoff from the Goodwood Revival in England. The expatriate Russian had been running his C-type Jaguar at the vintage racing meet and St. Scot had been there as a guest of Jaguar to cover the event. They had become quick, if unlikely, friends. St. Scot had even steered him in the direction of Terrance Filby when Portunoff was in the market for an original Allard J2 sports racing car. St. Scot had made fenders for Filby's Allard years earlier, back before Mort Welsh had taken over all of the metal fabricating for Filby's collection.

Portunoff's letter was, like the man himself, charming.

```
Simon:
I trust this note finds you well. I had a bit
of a problem a few weeks ago at the vintage
race at Lime Rock Park in Connecticut. You
know how we race hard in England? Well, com-
ing into Big Bend I never expected that the
guy in the Lister Jaguar would lift to let
```

me through and I hit the back of him with the
front fender of my Allard. I made a bit of
a mess of it too, I'm afraid. Not the other
car, which just barely had a scratch, but I'm
afraid I really did in the poor old Allard's
front fender. I was going to ship the car back
to England for repairs, when I remembered that
you were the one who made these fenders for
Filby. I thought I would send the car to you
and you could fix the fender, or make a new one,
if you're interested. I have a buyer lined up
for the Allard, so time is pretty tight. Can
you do it? Please ring me up when you get this.
   By the way, don't you answer your e-mails
anymore? Cheers! Portunoff

St. Scot smiled sourly at that part about the e-mail. His virus-damaged computer was still at the computer repair shop and its prospects weren't good. He still had Portunoff's phone number in England and, looking at his watch, reasoned that the Russian was probably still up. He made the call.

"Portunoff here."

"Yes Vladimir. It's Simon St. Scot calling."

"Ah, Simon. You got my letter then?" At least Portunoff's Russian accent was real.

"Yes, Vladimir. Sorry to hear about your Allard, but I guess these things happen..."

"Exactly the right attitude, my friend! So can I send my poor car over and have you fix it?"

"Well, I still have the pressboard patterns in my workshop from the first set I made for Terry Filby, so it should be pretty easy." He thought about the mess he was in, but maybe working on the old race car would take his mind off of things. "Sure, send it over, I'll be waiting for it."

"Great! It will be shipped tomorrow."

For the next two days St. Scot busied himself finishing up the Cadillac story and the piece on the Wilden Mysteria. The staff kept out of his way and Blinsky just scowled at him. Late Friday evening a large, enclosed car transporter pulled up in front of St. Scot's firehouse. Inside was Portunoff's gleaming red Allard sports car. The right front fender was crushed badly. St. Scot helped the delivery guy unload the car and they pushed it through the front doors and to the back where St. Scot did his metalworking.

Even damaged, the car looked brutish and aggressive. Allards had always been among St. Scot's favorite sports cars of the early 1950s and the J2 was the top of the breed. After the transporter drove off, St Scot locked up the doors of the firehouse and went upstairs to his loft and went to bed. It had been a long, tiring week.

The next morning, St. Scot set to work removing the fender and the brackets from the right front of the Cadillac-engined British monster. In the 50's, Sydney Allard had built a run of the brutish minimal roadsters, usually powered by large American V-8 engines. Some had flathead Fords, others had Chrysler Hemis, but the fastest had engines that were originally designed to power heavy Cadillac sedans. Stuffed into a lightweight roadster the engines must have felt like they had gone to heaven. The cars were scary and exciting to watch and even more so to drive. For a long time the cars of Sydney Allard had only a small following, but being featured at the Monterey Historic Races had brought them to the attention of collectors. The values of the cars had gone up considerably, and the J2 model was now well into six figures.

It was surprisingly easy to make new parts for the car. In fact, an Allard was such a simple car that it wouldn't be hard for a metal fabricator to build up a whole car from scratch. Cadillac and Chrysler engines were readily available and the rest of the chassis and suspension could practically be thrown together from scrap iron by a clever blacksmith.

St. Scot knew he wasn't the first to think of this and, as with counterfeit masterpieces in the art world, a number of fake so-called "air cars" had appeared from time to time. This was especially a problem for really high-end racing cars from small manufacturers like Bugatti and Ferrari. The cars had been virtually hand-made, so having an unscrupulous craftsman build one out of thin air wasn't too difficult. St. Scot knew of an old story that of the thirty-nine Ferrari 250 GTO sports racing cars built in the early 1960s, only about seventy still survive.

After St. Scot had removed the fender he looked at it carefully. He sorted through the stack of wooden patterns in his cabinet until he found the correct one. The fender itself had been made from a flat sheet of steel and had been rolled and shaped on the English wheel until the right shape had been achieved. A bead of wire was rolled into the edges to finish them off. St. Scot looked at the pattern and then looked at the fender. Something didn't seem quite right. He took out his measuring tape and carefully measured the damaged part and compared it to his pattern. *It didn't look right because it wasn't right!* Carefully, St. Scot felt along the crushed beaded edge for the three small scribe notches he always placed on his work. Like many craftsman, he felt enormous pride in seeing his handiwork at car shows or on the racetrack and the almost invisible notches were his secret way for cars he worked on to always carry a part of him with them. Now, running his finger along the trailing edge of the fender, he couldn't feel the three aligned notches. Pulling out a magnifying glass, he examined the fender very carefully. The workmanship was exceptional, better in fact than the car would have had when it was new. Better in fact than St. Scot knew he was capable of. Someone else had fabricated the fender. St. Scot paused for a moment, feeing the by now familiar sense of dread, but then dismissed it as paranoia and an overworked imagination. He tried to shrug it off. Portunoff had asked him to fix his broken racing car, and that's what he would do. Still...

St. Scot checked his watch. It was late in the evening in England, but St. Scot decided to make a phone call and at least leave a message for Portunoff.

The Russian answered the phone on the first ring. When St. Scot told him about the fender, Vladimir Portunoff's reaction was one of incomprehension. "What do you mean it's not your fender?" he said. "Of course it is! It is the car I bought from your Terrance Filby's collection. The one you made the fenders for. It hasn't been used since I bought it, just stored and then made ready for the Lime Rock race."

"I've made wooden templates for all of the cars I've ever worked on and the fender of the Allard simply doesn't match the template," St. Scot stated firmly.

After a few seconds of silence Vladimir asked, ""Have you checked the other three fenders?"

"No, hold on a minute." Several long minutes passed before he returned to the phone.

"Vladimir," St. Scot said slowly, "this Allard's a fake."

CHAPTER 17

St. Scot was fifteen minutes late when he walked into the magazine office on Monday morning. He had uncharacteristically overslept after his alarm hadn't sounded. He'd forgotten to set it, which was out of character, too. The receptionist told him that the editorial meeting had already started in the conference room in back and St. Scot went straight across the empty large area of the building and walked through the open door and into the meeting room. Blinsky was standing at the head of the table and the staff was seated around the large conference table.

"Ah, Mr. St. Scot, how nice of you to join us," said Blinsky venomously. "Please be seated, and next time try to be on time," he added curtly.

St. Scot found a chair next to Jopp.

"As I was saying," Blinsky continued, "There are two ways in which I am going to make this magazine profitable. The first is to cut expenses. There has been far too much fun here at the company's expense. It is time to be serious. WPI has already begun looking for buyers for this monstrosity of a building."

The faces around the table looked numb.

Blinsky continued. "But we can help, too. Look around you at all of this art," Blinsky pointed to some of the antique posters on the walls, "and to these books," his arm swept across to encompass the bookshelves behind him. "With everything on the internet today, we don't need this kind of overhead and there are plenty of book collectors who would be happy to buy these. I want someone from the art department to go through these books and artwork and make a list that I can give to WPI for items that we can sell."

Several people shifted uncomfortably in their chairs.

"The other way in which we can help is to make sure that our stories have real relevance," Blinsky continued. "By relevance, I mean that they will help sell advertising. It's an area that Terrance Filby just didn't understand, but one that will be the cornerstone of our magazine."

Blinsky was starting to fall into his faux-Russian count act again.

"We can bring this magazine back from the brink, with me as your leader! Do as you are told and you will make me a success at WPI. And when I am a success, you too will all be successful!"

All Blinsky got from the assembled staff of the magazine was a stony silence. Nobody said anything. Nobody looked at anyone else. Each was lost in his or her own sense of dread and despair. Blinsky, then nodded to the staff, oblivious to the obvious lack of morale, scooped up his stack of papers and walked out of the room.

By noon, Jopp had tendered his resignation. He stopped in to see St. Scot on his way out the door. St. Scot told him that he was doing the right thing and gave him a contact to call at the competition across town. St. Scot wasn't worried about Jopp. He would have another job before sundown. St. Scot only wished he could go with him. The rest of the staff was quiet and subdued and the only silver lining that St. Scot could see in Blinsky's bizarre "pep talk" was that it had focused everyone's animosity away from him and toward their new common enemy, at least for the time being.

Late in the afternoon Blinsky called St. Scot into his office. He was reading a newspaper when St. Scot walked in, motioned to a chair across the desk from him and continued to read for another full minute. St. Scot just sat and waited.

Putting down the paper and shaking his head sadly, Blinsky said, "Simon, I am very disappointed in you. You have already been undermining my authority with the staff. Winston Marshfield warned me that this would happen, but I told him my good friend Simon would never do such a thing. I guess I was wrong." Blinsky let the statement hang there like a dark cloud in the room.

St. Scot started to speak but Blinsky cut him off.

"Don't bother trying to deny it. Jopp told me he was leaving and that you had encouraged him to do so," Blinsky continued. "Simon, I don't know what to do with you, how to get through to you. Why would you go and see Winston Marshfield? Do you understand that he has enough on you to ruin your career and possibly put you in prison for a long time? The only reason he hasn't done so is because I have asked him not to. But maybe that doesn't mean anything to you, maybe we will have to get through to you in another less subtle way." Blinsky's eyes looked dark.

St. Scot just glared at Blinsky, not saying anything.

"And another thing. I got a visit from a police detective asking questions about you. I don't want to have my employees involved with police investigations. It's bad for business," Blinsky said. Suddenly, his mood brightened. "Well, anyway, I will just have to see what we will do. In the meanwhile I have to go to New York for a meeting and I want you to go to Road America on the Porsche trip. Jopp was supposed to go, but obviously he can't now." Blinsky looked pleased that he was making command decisions. "You can go now Simon, but please try to remember that we do have more persuasive ways of making you play the game our way."

With that Blinsky picked up his newspaper and began reading again. St. Scot sat in his chair for several seconds.

"Ivan," he started, talking to the raised newspaper. "I don't know what you and Marshfield think you have on me, and I don't know what you both plan to gain from all of this, but I want you to know something," St. Scot's voice remained firm. "I am not now nor have I ever been your friend. I will find my way out of this situation and I will find a way to make you and Marshfield and anyone else who is involved in this pay. Do you understand me?"

St. Scot was standing now, his fists clenched at his sides. From behind the raised newspaper he heard Blinsky sigh.

Then, curtly, with almost no emotion came the words, "You may go now."

St. Scot turned and stalked out of the office.

CHAPTER 18

Road America in Elkhart Lake, Wisconsin is perhaps the most beautiful racetrack in the country. It is one of the oldest, dating from the early 1950s, and is certainly the longest at just over four miles per lap. St. Scot had raced at Road America many times, often in his own Turner or pre-War Riley vintage racing cars. The track itself was a wonderful technical challenge for a driver, but almost on par with that as a drawing card, was the food. The concessions were run by various civic groups from the nearby resort town of Elkhart Lake and they vied with one another to make the best possible food, the most famous of which was bratwurst grilled on an open fire. It could be prepared almost any way you wanted it, but St. Scot preferred the purist brat on a roll slathered in hot mustard. On a brisk fall day, with the leaves changing and the smells of brats cooking on a charcoal fire, mixed with the heady aroma of several hundred vintage racing cars, it was hard to imagine a better place to be.

St. Scot arrived in Milwaukee late in the afternoon and was met by a shuttle from Porsche. Since he was one of the last of the journalists to arrive, the driver threw the light overnight bag into the cargo space of his minivan and invited St. Scot to ride up front with him. The drive through Milwaukee's rush hour was tedious, made more so by an accident on the freeway just north of the airport, and it was more than two hours later when he finally arrived at the American Inn in Kohler. Arriving just as dinner orders were being taken, St. Scot found a seat next to Porsche's head of Public Relations. There were about a dozen journalists in the room and St. Scot was by far the most senior magazine representative. He couldn't help thinking that this would have been a perfect trip for Jopp, who was still making a name for himself among his peers. Oh, well. No doubt he'd do fine wherever he landed. It was a small enough group that Porsche hadn't set the menu so St. Scot started with a radicchio, mushroom and endive salad with walnut vinaigrette dressing, followed by pecan-crusted walleye with potatoes au gratin. Dinner made up for the long day of travel.

The dinner conversation was light and centered on Porsche's prospects in the upcoming sports car racing series. Eschewing dessert, St. Scot turned in early, leaving the younger crowd to smoke cigars and drink expensive single malt scotch at Porsche's considerable expense.

Morning came early and after demolishing most of eastern Wisconsin's supply of eggs, bacon, ham, orange juice, coffee, pancakes and waffles, the ravenous group of automotive journalists were ready to board Porsche's bus for the short trip to Road America. Even with an ample breakfast, St. Scot's mouth began to water as the bus drove through the track gates and he began thinking about bratwurst. Fortunately, Porsche had plenty more pastries and coffee available upon the group's arrival, and at least in the short term, nobody seemed in imminent danger of starving to death.

The day started out with a classroom session that covered both the improvements that had been made to the previous year's Porsches and also how to negotiate the challenging Road America circuit. There really wasn't that much difference between last year's and this year's models, more of a continuous evolution of what was already an amazing automobile: a bit more horsepower, a slight recalibration of the dynamic stability system, slightly better brakes, each improvement bringing the cars closer and closer to the always unattainable perfection. After the classroom session it was time to strap on a helmet and join an instructor for some familiarization laps before Porsche let the group of journalists loose with a dozen expensive sports cars on a wide open racetrack.

St. Scot found himself paired with one of Porsche's professional racers, a driver he knew well. Instead of getting into the driver's side to provide some demonstration laps, the racer pointed to St. Scot and said, "You drive, hot-shoe."

St. Scot smiled. He had driven with the man before on other events and had even raced against him at a vintage race a few years ago. Now the pro-driver was paying a compliment to his driving skills. St. Scot adjusted his driving position, fired up the engine and slid the lever for the six-speed manual gearbox into first. He slowly rumbled out of the pits, giving the engine and gearbox a chance to warm-up before he started driving fast. After about half a lap he began to open up the throttle and felt the car surge forward.

"I think you'll find it more fun with the electronics shut off," the man said from the passenger seat as he reached over and pushed a button that turned off the Porsche's traction control and dynamic stability programs.

The car was every bit as good as St. Scot remembered and he began working the brakes and the tires as he drove deeper and deeper into the corners. It was nothing like driving a vintage racer where everything was a compromise. In the Porsche he could use all of the braking, all of the tires' formidable grip, all of the engine's fabulous horsepower to hammer his way around the track. Once in a while he would glance over at the racer in the passenger seat, who was sitting calmly with arms and legs relaxed and a slight smile on his face. After a dozen laps, St. Scot felt like he had reached a plateau and drove the sports car into the pit lane.

"Your turn," said St. Scot.

He and the racing champion changed places and the pro took the car onto the track, showing St. Scot a few places where he was losing a bit of time and giving him an idea where he could cut a few tenths off his lap times. They spent the morning like this, swapping the wheel back and forth and St. Scot marveled at the quiet professionalism and the ability of the man to teach the nuances of performance driving. St. Scot had always liked the Porsche Carrera Coupe. It was powerful and relatively easy to drive and was built like a brick shithouse. The cars were so solid that they were used in Porsche's own driving schools with no modifications and no problems.

Finally, the checkered flag was displayed and they headed for the pits and to the lunch of grilled bratwurst that Porsche had arranged at the track. It had been a glorious morning and now it was topped off by a perfect lunch. Two of the Porsches had been damaged so far in the morning's drive. In both cases it had been by relatively inexperienced journalists who had decided to turn off the stability management system to see what the cars were like without the assistance of the electronic wizardry. Both had lost control on the tricky and very fast kink section of the racing circuit. Nobody was injured but both cars were crunched and unusable. One of the guilty drivers was so disconsolate that he didn't want to eat his bratwurst, but the other was unconcerned enough that he ate enough to make up the shortfall in Porsche's undoubtedly precise bratwurst predictions. St. Scot ate his with hot mustard and relish and then bid a genuinely fond farewell to the Porsche executives. What a car. What a job. What a life. He had an early flight and the nice folks from Porsche had a minivan waiting to take him to the airport in Milwaukee.

While waiting for his flight at the airport, St. Scot fired up his cell phone and checked his messages. There were two messages from Mark Summers. St. Scot smiled. With his Managing Editor trying again to reach him, maybe his life was returning back to normal.

The next message was an hour and a half old and was from his alarm security company. They were informing him that the heat and smoke detectors at his firehouse home had gone off and that since they hadn't been able to reach him to confirm it was a false alarm, they were going to notify the fire department.

CHAPTER 19

From a block away, St. Scot could see a couple of fire trucks and a police car parked in front of his old firehouse. The late afternoon sunlight peaked through a light smoky haze that hung over the neighborhood. At first he thought everything was going to be all right. He was wrong. As he came closer he noticed that most of the upper story windows were broken and black streaks smudged the exterior walls of the building. A small crowd was milling in front. He parked his Chrysler 300 press car at one of the barricades, walked up to a policeman and identified himself as the owner of the building. A thin trail of smoke was still rising from two or three of the windows and there was the acrid smell of burning rubber. The policeman called over to someone on his walkie-talkie and a fireman walked over to St. Scot and then led him into the smoldering remains of his home.

Inside, the floors were covered with water. The air was heavy with smoke and steam. Everything was coated in a thick black residue. Light was dimly filtering through the soot-coated windows that still remained. But the most devastating view of all were the charred hulks that were once his modest collection of old sports and racing cars. The MGA he had driven so recently was a black pile of metal sitting on four charred and tire-less wire wheels. The leather interior was completely burned away. The heat had blackened and cracked the windshield and all of the paint had charred and burned off of the once cheer-ful red roadster. The room's overhead lights had come crashing down from the ceiling and there were tangled masses of wiring entwined around the other debris. At the far end of the room, his English wheel, by some miracle, sat seemingly untouched above the melted and destroyed examples of his metal fab-rication work. The fire had been intense enough to melt the aluminum fenders he had so recently worked on, and all of his wooden metal-working tools had become cinders, including the wooden patterns he had made over the years. There was nothing left. As the fireman led him toward the front of the building St. Scot looked upward at the second floor where he once lived. The fireman shook his head, indicating it wouldn't be safe to go up and, at the same time, letting him know that there wouldn't be any more to see.

As he emerged from the building, St. Scot was met by De-tective Jameson. She was dressed in a severely cut business suit and it was clear she wasn't in a good mood.

"Ah, Mr. St. Scot," she said. "Might I have a word with you?"

St. Scot, who was feeling a bit dizzy from everything he'd just seen, nodded wearily. "You'll forgive me if I don't offer you anything," he mumbled.

Jameson ignored him and went on. "I have been assigned to this case. The fire investigator has already been in the build-ing and says there were four separate ignition points. I don't have his official report yet, but that will make it a clear case of arson."

"I see," said St. Scot nodding numbly.

"Can you tell me, Mr. St. Scot, who besides yourself had access to the building? Who else had a set of keys? Who might have wanted to do this?"

St. Scot thought for a few seconds. Who would want to do him harm? That was the question he had been trying to answer for the better part of the last two weeks.

"What do you mean who had keys?" asked St. Scot slowly.

Jameson looked at him carefully before answering. "Mr. St . Scot, the fire department came because they were called by your alarm company after the smoke detectors went off. But, prior to that, there was no alarm caused by an illegal entry. Assuming you had properly set your alarm, it appears that someone who had a key must have come into the building and set the fires. Who besides you had a key?"

St. Scot shook his head. "The only other person with a key besides me is the neighbor girl who waters my plants. She lives down the street and her name is Allison Chalmers."

Jameson wrote the name in her notebook. Something was nagging at the back of St. Scot's mind. *Blinsky! He had given Blinsky a key when he had stayed with him a few nights ago. Had he given the key back?* St. Scot hesitated before saying, "Actually my boss at the magazine has a key, too. He stayed here a few nights ago. His name is Ivan Blinsky, you remember we talked about him before? I don't know where he's living right now."

Jameson nodded her head and wrote down Blinsky's name in her notebook. She then turned and spoke briefly to one of the firemen and then, turning back asked, "Mr. St. Scot, would you mind walking through the building again and telling me what used to be here?"

St. Scot winced, reluctant to go back inside, but knew that he had to. Together they walked into the wrecked building and St. Scot pointed out the various still-smoking shapes. "This is, or rather used to be, a 1929 Chrysler Model 72 Sport Roadster. It was done up in the style of the cars that were so successful that year at the 24-Hour race at Le Mans," he began.

The object he pointed to was charred and sagging. The heat had been so intense that the car's wooden frame had caught fire in places and burned through the metal coachwork. The usually proud chrome grille had turned a rusty brown in the heat of the fire.

They walked to the next car. "This had been a 1959 Porsche 356 Coupe. There wasn't anything really special about it except it had been my father's car and he had truly loved it." The Porsche had been a resplendent ivory white. Now it was a smeary rust and soot color and the heat from the fire had blown out the windows of the little sports car. St. Scot remembered all of the trips to sports car races he and his father had made together in the little car while St. Scot was growing up. Now it was a burned out hulk. A lump caught in his throat.

Jameson made sympathetic noises about the Porsche and it was clear she understood the magnitude of his loss. They moved down the line. "This is my 1949 MG TC. Again, not such a special car, but one that I really did enjoy driving." St. Scot looked over the badly burned car, once one of the better TC's in the country. He had entered it in two major Concours and had come away with a Best in Class and a People's Choice award. Its exposed slab of a gas tank had obviously exploded outward, blowing apart the whole back half of the car and helping to spread the fire more quickly. The MG was beyond salvaging. "I guess it's a goner," he said quietly.

"The next car here is a 1958 Turner vintage racing car. Quite rare. Coventry Climax engine. Fun car to race." His mind drifted back to the previous summer when he had raced the car last. He had done well, fighting with an Elva Courier for most of a feature race to finish ninth out of twenty-six. The fiber-glass body of the Turner had melted into a blackened mass on the firehouse floor. The poor little car wold never race again.

Near the center of the room, where the fire had obviously been the most intense, were the barely recognizable charred remains of a Chris Craft speedboat. Built in the 1950s, with dual cockpits, the boat had been one of St. Scot's pride and joys. He had rebuilt the 283-cubic inch Chevrolet engine himself and had enjoyed gracefully cruising the waterways on Sunday afternoon's with the stylish craft. For the brief time that they were together, it had been Elizabeth's favorite in all of his collection of toys. Now you could hardly tell that the pile of smoking wood sitting on its trailer had been a sleek and powerful vintage speedboat. Even the police detective seemed affected by the magnitude of what she was seeing.

And so it went. A few more racers, a couple of big pre-War cars. St. Scot's taste in old cars had always been varied and eclectic and the cars he owned weren't chosen for their investment value, but because they interested him.

At the back of the workshop, St. Scot pointed out the cabinet that had held all of his metal-working patterns. All at once it struck him. *Where was Portunoff's Allard?* When he left for Road America it had been parked right here, in front of the

English wheel. Even with the intensity of the fire, the charred remains should still be here. Yet there was no sign of the 1950s British sports car.

Detective Jameson looked at him. "What's the matter, Mr. St. Scot?"

St. Scot was startled she was still next to him.

"One of the cars is missing," he said finally. "It isn't my car, it belongs to a friend and I was doing some work on it for him. Before I left, the car was right here, and now it doesn't seem to be here anymore."

With no particular clues to look at, the detective took down the information about the Allard and its owner Mr. Portunoff. Then Jameson and St. Scot looked over each of the cars again to confirm that only the Allard was missing. Finally, they returned to the MGA at the front door. St. Scot was feeling numb by the loss he had suffered and by the unexplained missing sports car. The detective turned to him and for an instant St. Scot felt the sympathy for his loss peek out from her official police façade.

"Do you mind if I ask a personal question?" he asked the detective.

Jameson narrowed her gaze and said "If it's why I wouldn't have lunch with you, let's just say you aren't my type and drop it, okay?"

St. Scot shook his head. "No, no, that isn't it! That model car behind your desk, the one painted sort of pea green. What kind of car is that? I've been wracking my brain trying to identify it but I can't seem to place it."

Jameson almost smiled. "That is a Jameson Mark I. It was a racing car my father built in the 1950s and raced with some success. It was a one-off and before he died of cancer a couple of years ago he made a model of it to help me remember him," she said.

St. Scot nodded, looked around him and smiled sadly. "I had a few models of some of these cars too," he said, "but they were upstairs and from what the fireman told me, not much is left upstairs."

As he emerged from the building, Allison Chalmers detached herself from the small crowd out front, ran up and threw her arms around him. He hugged her back. Tears ran down her face as she looked over the mess.

"Simon, oh Simon. The plants, the cars, everything's all gone isn't it?" she asked in a voice filled with despair.

The sadness in the young girl's eyes made him want to cry. He reassured her that he would be all right and suddenly felt very tired. He knew it wasn't going to be all right. Ali held him tighter and began to cry harder. This old fire station with his collection of cars and metal working equipment, along with his job at the magazine, had been his life. He had surrounded himself with things and writing and cut himself off from people who he cared for or who might care for him. He had convinced himself that he didn't need anyone. He had learned to be content in his solitude. And now everything was gone. Detective Jameson backed away, leaving him in his grief. He stood there next to the smoldering ruin of his life, tears rolling down his cheeks as he held the slightly-built sobbing girl in his arms.

St. Scot spent the night at a local cut-rate hotel. He had met with his insurance agent at the firehouse after Allison's mother had finally arrived and detached her broken-hearted daughter from St. Scot's neck. It was clear that the arson word had already spread. The agent wasn't exactly specific on how long it would take to process a claim, but promised him that he would move as soon as the fire inspector's report was in his hands.

The next morning St. Scot pulled back on the same clothes he had worn the day before. They smelled of smoke, but the few things in his small overnight bag from the trip to Road America were now all the clothes that he owned. Even his beloved brown leather jacket was gone. He wheeled the Chrysler over to the magazine office and noticed that the parking lot was nearly full.

Pushing through the front doors the receptionist told him that the entire staff was already assembled in the conference room. St. Scot hurried back and found the room filled and Blinsky standing at the front holding court. Blinsky paused in his oration and gave St. Scot a look of pure hatred.

"Don't bother to sit down, Simon, you won't be staying that long." He looked at the staff and continued. "I have an announcement for everyone, and especially for you, Simon. As of right now, this minute, you are no longer employed by this magazine. Certain irregularities of a financial nature have come to light. It appears that Mr. St. Scot here has been accepting bribes and kickbacks from our advertisers and squirreling them away. I have evidence that on his most recent trip to Texas, for example, he accepted a large sum of money from Mr. Wilden in exchange for promises that we would promote his new sports car. I don't know if there will be any legal action taken, but I think we will all agree that it is best if Simon just leaves us quietly and right away. I expect you will clean out your desk and be gone within the hour, Mr. St. Scot."

PART 2

"Men who are indifferent to what they wear,
and are not terribly concerned with what they
eat, will make absurd sacrifices
to possess an automobile"
—Ken Purdy

CHAPTER 20

The late forties Ford F100 pickup truck slowed and pulled into the gravel driveway. It crunched along the short drive and pulled up in front of a weathered barn next to a small farmhouse. Simon St. Scot opened the door of the gray primer-painted vehicle and looked up at the sky. There was light snow in the forecast and the leaden skies were making the weatherman look good.

St. Scot had moved 80 miles away from his problems to the farm that had been left to him by his parents after they'd died together in a small-plane crash in Alaska twelve years earlier. With no job and no house, what were his options? Whoever had done this to him had been very thorough. Aside from Detective Jameson, who insisted on knowing his whereabouts for her ongoing investigations, he had only told Allison where he was going. Allison had helped him load the English wheel into the pickup and before he drove off she hugged him fiercely.

Because the fire was definitely arson, the insurance company was dragging its feet about paying St. Scot anything for his losses. The company that insured his classic cars was waiting for the other company to pay on the building and its contents before they settled with St. Scot for his cars, and so there was no motion there either. The only good news was that although the building had been heavily damaged, the building inspector and insurance company had agreed it could be salvaged.

St. Scot had been fired from the magazine by Blinsky for what the WPI attorneys had called 'moral turpitude." St. Scot's severance package was marginal, but his attorney had advised him to take it with the condition that he would not sign anything that admitted any wrongdoing. This had stalemated his negotiation with his former employer, whose lawyers were perfectly happy to hold things up as long as possible, all the while charging their clients for the delays. So, until something happened there, St. Scot was going to have to live off of his savings and a few small investments. He'd always figured he should invest in something he knew about, and that something had been old cars. Instead of building a stock portfolio, he had started a small collection of classic automobiles. None of the cars in his firehouse could compare with those of Terrance Filby's, but he had a few—like his Nash Healey and a nice pre-War Riley Special that had some investor value. And the mahogany Chris Craft had been worth some real bucks. Now everything was gone, and with the insurance company questioning everyone about the reason for the blaze, nothing seemed like it was going to happen soon.

He had worked for the magazine for so long and was so used to having a different press car every night, he didn't own any modern transportation. The only of St. Scot's treasures that hadn't been destroyed in the fire was the old Ford truck that he'd recently sent to the body shop to be repainted. Retrieving the old truck from the paint shop, he'd had Ali help him load the remarkably unburned and still usable English metal working wheel from his firehouse workshop into the truck bed, though taking even this one item had been a fight with his insurers, and driven out to the farm. He was sick of the whole mess and actually felt relieved to be leaving everything behind for awhile.

He needed a plan, one that included revenge. The problem was where to start? He still didn't know who his enemies were or if he had any friends.

It took St. Scot almost two weeks to re-open the small house and clean out the barn. Years of neglect were evident and St. Scot felt bad about having letting the place his parents had chosen to retire to fall into such disrepair. They had bought the small farm two years before they went on the Alaska adventure, but had actually spent very little time there. The farmhouse was a traditional two-story with a parlor, dining room, living room and half bath downstairs and two bedrooms and a full bath upstairs. There were still unopened boxes of his mother's clothes and his parent's memories in the spare bedroom.

The barn had been his father's domain and was dry and snug, although evicting a well-established and very respectable family of raccoons had been a trial. Without Ali's help, St. Scot now needed a block and tackle to unload the English wheel into his father's workshop in the corner of the barn, not far from the old wood stove that provided heat for working on projects in the wintertime. His father had been an engineer of the old school, the kind of man who intuitively understood complex mechanical systems and could instantly find ways to make them better. After thirty years at General Dynamics, he had taken an early retirement and set himself up as a consultant. His hobbies had only peripherally included auto-mobiles, although when he was younger he had enjoyed taking Simon to the sports car races in his old Porsche coupe. Flying had consumed much of his spare time, an interest he had passed on to Simon when he was younger. But the elder St. Scot's real passion had been complex and intricate machining, a talent he had also tried to instill in his son as he was growing up. Although not as skilled a machinist as his father, Simon had many of the skills and he was comfortable making and machining tools and parts.

Before he had died, St. Scot's father had insulated and weather-proofed the old farm building and had set up a machine shop with metal lathes and planing machines and several high-end gas-electric welding machines. He would occasionally make parts for St. Scot when he needed to restore one of his old cars. One thing Simon had done a dozen years ago, when he was closing the house and barn, was to carefully wrap all of his father's tools and machines in oily rags and waterproof plastic. Since moving to the farm, and with nothing better to do, St. Scot had been unpacking all of the machines and tools and reorganizing the shop.

It was hard moving into his parent's old house and it made him realize just how much he missed them. During the past years he had convinced himself that he was far too busy to let such feelings interfere with his life but now, with nothing but time on his hands, he was acutely aware that they were gone. Working in his dad's barn workshop was made doubly hard by a constant reminder of the kind of relationship he had enjoyed with his father. Tucked away in the back corner of the barn was a 1930 deHavilland DH60 Gypsy Moth biplane. St. Scot's father had bought the biplane and completely restored it, adding only the minimum amount of modern radios and avionics that would allow him to fly cross-country in crowded airspaces.

Just before leaving for his fatal trip to Alaska, St. Scot's dad had put the Gypsy Moth into storage in the barn, carefully wrapping the fabric wings and fuselage in plastic and draining the oil and fuel tanks. The British-built pilot trainer was incredibly reliable and easy to fly. It was the same kind of craft that Sir Francis Chichester had flown to Australia from England in 1929. Amy Johnson had done the same trip, also in a Gypsy Moth, in 1930 in 19 days, to become the first woman to make such a long distance flight alone. The biplane was strong and hearty and loads of fun to fly. St. Scot had even learned some basic aerobatics with the Gypsy Moth. It was perfectly safe doing all kinds of snap rolls and loops, as pioneer American aviatrix Laura Ingalls had proven in 1930 when she had flown 344 loops in a row, setting a record.

Of the thousands of Gypsy Moths built in the early 1930s, fewer than twenty were still flying. The elder St. Scot had taught his son the virtues of low and slow flight in the machine. St. Scot had later gone on to get a multi-engine rating, but quickly tired of the regimentation of modern aircraft piloting. When he needed to go somewhere, he took a commercial airliner. When he wanted to fly, he went up in the Gypsy Moth.

Standing in the dim recesses of the barn, his hand gently stroking the varnished wooden propeller, he remembered flying with his dad to Oshkosh for the experimental aircraft fly-in. The 100-horsepower four-cylinder Gypsy engine could push the little Moth to 100-mph when needed, but he and his dad had lazed along at 70-mph, occasionally buzzing a herd of cattle or a farmer working in his field. They had brought sleeping bags and a small tent in the cramped biplane and had barnstormed their way to and from Wisconsin in the best tradition of the Roaring Twenties. They slept under the airplane's wings at local airports and hitched rides into small towns to eat at genuine greasy spoon diners. It had been a trip into the past that St. Scot would never forget, much like those trips to the races in his dad's little Porsche —the Porsche that had now been reduced to ashes and melted metal.

The people of Addison County didn't seem to care one way or another about Simon St. Scot's arrival from the big city. Lucas Sonderson, the burly farmer who leased most of the farm's forty acres to grow corn, was a widower and a man of very few words. He shook his head slowly when St. Scot asked him if anyone did metal repair work in the area. St. Scot printed up a simple one-page sheet and distributed it among the farms and posted it around town. Almost immediately it resulted in two welding repair jobs to old tractors and farm equipment. It would be a meager income, but at least it might keep him busy.

Sometimes, when watching television in the evening or reading a magazine, he would find himself recognizing a place he had been in Europe or Asia on an automotive press trip. He had been at the top of his profession and it was difficult to accept that he wasn't there anymore. Was it shallow of him to miss the free business class tickets to Tokyo? Was it wrong for him to miss a ride in Ford's corporate jet to the west coast? Had he really needed that many Ferrari test drives in his life?

Was Monaco during the Grand Prix as grand as he remembered? Was it really that much fun to thrash a vintage Jaguar around a racetrack while its owner looked on with pride? Was the foie gras at Le Pyramid in Lyon really that good? The free food, the free cars, the free trips. God, did he miss it.

The one thing he absolutely didn't miss was his mail. Most days now, he was lucky if a sales flyer from the local farmer's feed supply store arrived at his mailbox. Allison Chalmers had written to him three times. Her letters were very business-like and serious while at the same time compassionate about the loss of his home and job. She had found job as a receptionist and was very excited about that. There was an undercurrent in her letters that St. Scot couldn't quite identify but that sometimes made the hairs on the back of his neck stand up in warning. She was so young and vulnerable. Her son Ronnie was growing up quickly and St. Scot kept a picture of him on his refrigerator door. St. Scot had written a quick note back to Ali with a photograph of his farmhouse and barn.

Vladimir Portunoff had been strangely silent about the missing Allard, but with all of the other things that had happened to him, St. Scot had been just as happy not to hear from the Russian. Portunoff had lost a single car. St. Scot had lost his entire collection, his home, his job and the life that he had loved. It was strange that the car was missing but it was hard for St. Scot to feel much sympathy for Portunoff's plight. Still, when the old farmhouse telephone rang one night, St. Scot had been glad to hear it was Portunoff.

"Simon, my friend. Sorry to hear about your losses," the Russian boomed over the phone line.

"Vladimir, thank you. It's been pretty awful," St. Scot said lamely.

"Yes, yes, yes. Listen, I have something I want to talk with you about, but I'd rather do so in person. Can you pick me up at the airport tomorrow?"

Portunoff's flight from Heathrow landed in the late afternoon. St. Scot was waiting for him in the parking lot, standing next to his beat up old pickup truck.

"No more Porsches, Mister Journalist?" Portunoff asked smiling.

St. Scot shook Vladimir's hand and threw his overnight bag into the pickup bed. "I'm traveling undercover," he said with an exaggerated wink.

With heavy traffic and a slow old truck it took almost two hours to drive out to the farm. On the way, St. Scot filled Portunoff on his new life as a handyman.

"Sounds like the perfect vacation for you, Simon. But now maybe it's time to get to work and find the fiends that did this to you, and I think I can help," Portunoff said.

"Really?" St. Scot said quickly, turning his head to look at Portunoff. "How?"

"We'll come to that presently. I need to know more about what exactly happened. But not just yet." With that, Portunoff shifted his body on the trucks decrepit bench seat and took a nap for the remainder of the trip.

They arrived at St. Scot's farm and together went straight out to the barn. Vladimir looked at the machine shop and the English wheel with an approving glance.

"Nice setup you have here," he said. After a pause, Portunoff got right to the point. "So, what evidence did you have that my Allard wasn't right?"

St. Scot shook his head slowly. "Vladimir, there wasn't anything all that conclusive; it was more of a feeling I got when I looked at how the car was put together and how everything fit. For example," he continued, "the bolt used to hold the fender bracket to the frame. It looked like an old bolt. It had no markings, so we can't say how old it is. The head itself, the part you could see looked old and well used, but what you didn't see unless you take it apart, were the threads. They were clean and fresh. It wasn't much, but something just wasn't right about that. Then of course there was the matter that the fenders didn't match my original patterns and didn't have my identifying notches on them."

"Notches? What are those?"

"Well, every time I build something, I put some tiny identifying marks on it. They are pretty much invisible, but I know that they're there and it makes me feel like they're my contribution to history, or something. I know it's silly, but…"

Portunoff was silent for a few minutes and then nodded his head. "Yes, and those patterns, they were all consumed in the fire, no?" asked the Russian.

He then pulled a thick leather bound book from the soft briefcase he had carrying with him since getting off of the airliner. St. Scot recognized it as one of the individual histories that both he and Borgenson had worked on for Terrance Filby's collection of classic automobiles. This particular one was for the car that Portunoff had purchased from Filby. The Allard. It was written by Borgenson.

Portunoff slowly leafed through the pages. The book showed the car's early history, racing first in New England and later in the Midwest. It showed the restoration that took place more than twenty years earlier. The fenders that had been made for the car during that phase of its life had been poorly done and that was why, when Terry Filby got the car, he had asked St. Scot to make a new and correct set of fenders.

After a moment, Portunoff set the book down and said sadly, "So I bought a forgery. A fake." The Russian continued, "After buying this car from Terrance Filby, I have been brokering other cars that were in his collection. You know many of his cars went to Japan in the early 1990s. The Japanese were buying so many cars, they had so much money, and Terrance helped me find other cars to sell. We made good money." Vladimir looked wistful. "Those cars went to Japan and we never thought that any would ever return. Anyway, with the Japanese financial crisis there are suddenly a lot of cars, really very good cars, available. Since the fall of the Soviet Union there are also a fair number of super rich men in Russia who have an eye for really high quality goods. Not just cars, but all kinds of artwork. They are buying, my friend. They are buying with cold, hard American currency. And, they are buying through me. "

St. Scot asked, "the Russian Mafia?"

Portunoff shrugged. "That is one name for them. There is, what you might say, a thriving import and export business in my home country right now. Maybe you heard about the recent shipment of windshield washer fluid from the U.S. that was actually blue-tinted grain alcohol? Remove the tinting, add some flavoring and voila! Instant vodka. Art, machine tools, chemicals, weapons, women, drugs, you name it. The amount of money being made is staggering. We Russians like our luxuries. Oh, I know in the west you still think of us as down trodden and oppressed peasants, but I am telling you there are plenty who like the finer things. And now, some have the money to buy them. Anyway, being a Russian by birth, I have been, shall we say, helping these men find and buy some exceptional cars. The Japanese seem more than willing to work with me and most of the cars have this kind of provenance."

Portunoff pointed to the still open Allard book. He looked uneasy. "The people I have sold these cars to will not be as charitable as I am about having purchased a fake. There could be real trouble here Simon, real trouble."

St. Scot and his Russian guest drove into town for dinner at the local pizza place. Thick crust, pepperoni, mushrooms and sausage washed down with Canadian beer. After three pieces each, Vladimir asked St. Scot to tell him, in as much detail as he could recall, the events leading to his dismissal from the magazine and his new life as country squire and general handyman.

"It all started when Filby and Borgenson were fired at the magazine," began St. Scot.

Portunoff interrupted. "Are you so sure that's when it started? You are only looking at the story that you know. Use your journalist sense, when did the story really begin?"

St. Scot hesitated. "I suppose it started when Borgenson and I started writing those history books for Terrance Filby."

"And why do you say that?"

"Well, I didn't realize it at the time, but by so carefully documenting everything that was known about each individual car, we were sort of setting up a blueprint how to make forgeries of them."

"Go on."

"Well, if Bill and I so meticulously described all of the intimate details of each car then, if you were counterfeiting one of the cars, you would know exactly what details were likely to be checked during any authentication."

"Excellent! Continue."

St. Scot shifted uneasily. "But then that means that Terrance Filby…"

Portunoff leaned forward. "That Terrance Filby was the one doing the forgery? I have come to the same conclusion, but through other channels. But leave that for a moment and continue your story."

"So Filby and Borgenson get fired…" St. Scot began again.

"No, not yet, too soon," the Russian interrupted. "Tell me what happened before then."

St. Scot thought. "Well," he said, "WPI bought the magazine."

"And who is WPI?" asked Portunoff.

"Um, some sort of conglomerate. Big into all kinds of things. They are heavily connected in places like Russia…" It was if a light bulb suddenly appeared over St. Scot's head. A dim one, but a light bulb nonetheless.

"Yes. In fact, I am WPI. Or part of it. One of its directors actually," said Portunoff. "Simon, my friend," he continued, "you Americans just don't do intrigue as well as we Russians. Do you know what I did before I moved to England? No? Not many know this, but let me tell you. I was an operations manager for the KGB. You know the KGB? Yes? Good. My specialty was disinformation. I was very good at this. We became very good at getting people in trouble with their jobs and their home life and then offering to fix it all if they would give us something in return. You understand this, yes?"

St. Scot nodded his head slowly.

"You might call it blackmail. To me it was my job. Okay, so I had enough one day and decided to defect. Oh, did I mention I had stored away lots of KGB money in some special bank accounts? Mainly in Switzerland?" The Russian looked pleased. "Anyway, I figured spending money in England would be more fun than spending money in Moscow. My timing was superb. I left Russia and the whole place fell apart. My Soviet Union fell apart. The information I had was no longer of any value to the British or Americans and the Russians never knew I was going to be a traitor to them." Portunoff looked happy. "As I was nobody's enemy I did the capitalist thing and started an import and export company in England. I was very good at it and it helped add to the fortune that I, shall we say, removed from the KGB. I tell you this now so that you will understand what I am about to tell you."

St. Scot was listening carefully.

"Some of my old associates at KGB decided to buy a legitimate company to help them look respectable. This was some years ago. They bought WPI and asked me to be a director. I said yes. For a long time I think it is a pretty good company. Honest, you know. But then some of us began to get some information about something we don't want to hear. Like, maybe crime."

St. Scot nodded. "Okay, so Filby and Borgenson got fired." He paused, expecting to be interrupted again by the Russian, but Portunoff remained silent. "Then Bill shot himself. Except it wasn't suicide. I know this because he sent me an e-mail the night he died. But then my computer caught a virus and is now out of action and the only copy of that e-mail is in the hands of the police. Meanwhile, Winston Marshfield told everyone that the changes at the magazine were my idea and Ivan Blinsky was put in charge. Then they torched my firehouse. Now everyone thinks I stole a bunch of money and maybe even murdered Bill Borgenson."

"My friend, Mister Journalist Simon St. Scot, I can't be sure, but it sounds like you have been setup with the kind of disinformation scam that I used to run for the KGB. They took your nice life, they took your job, they even took your home and the things you were passionate about, your cars. The computer was a nice touch, too. They probably infected it. Even when I was KGB we were beginning to work with computer viruses. Such things are not so difficult today. They did leave you alive, which was a bit sloppy, but somebody must have interceded on your behalf. They needed to get rid of you in a way that would leave you in disgrace, in a way that wouldn't let you come back and mess anything up. They did it rather well. As a professional, I salute them," Vladimir said raising his half-full glass of beer.

St. Scot shook his head. "Why would anyone do that?" he asked. "I have nothing that anyone would want."

Portunoff looked at him shrewdly. "Oh no, my friend? Then why am I, such an important man, no? Why am I here sitting with you in this pizza place in the middle of god-forsaken nowhere? You have knowledge. You have worked on several of Mr. Filby's cars, no? You had a position of respect and a way to talk to the world through the magazine you worked for. You also wrote some of these books that Terrance Filby uses to sell the authenticity of his cars. Isn't that right?"

St. Scot started to say something but Vladimir interrupted. "You also had those patterns and records in your workshop before it burned down. It seems to me, my friend, that you had information that could damage an operation like this."

St. Scot looked startled. "Do you mean you think there is more? More than just your Allard? How can that be? Who is running all of this?"

Portunoff looked thoughtful and deflected the question. "This man Blinsky, I know him. He has some connections to the men in Russia I speak about who buy cars from me. I think they feed him information sometimes for his stories. He is nobody, but I think that maybe he wants to be somebody. I am sure he is not important, but he may know who is. Marshfield of WPI. Yes, I know him. A very ambitious man, that one. He has friends in Russia who I used to work with in my KGB days. They could tell him how to do this to you, maybe even help him. Especially after what happened to you in New York, I think he may have put together something, or is working for someone else. He is connected to the right people for that. Marshfield certainly has the assets to arrange what has happened to you. Even to take care of Mr. Borgenson. He is the one we are watching, my associates and I."

The Russian was silent for a moment while he took another pull on his beer. Then he continued. "WPI is a very powerful company, especially now in Russia. Dangerous men are involved, capable of all this and more. We tried to keep it straight and honest but there is just too much money, so maybe our Mr. Marshfield has gone into business for himself. You don't need to know more than that now."

Portunoff looked very calm suddenly. "I don't know who is doing this. But I do know some of the men I have sold cars to in the past few years. I also know that if we both want to stay alive, and I do mean that as I said it, we had better find out who is behind all of this and what exactly they are doing. I need to know some things for sure, things that only you can tell me, and I know where I want you to start."

CHAPTER 21

St. Scot and Portunoff examined a list of cars that the Russian had sold over the past four years to rich collectors in the former Soviet Union. St. Scot looked at the list and the prices paid in awe. It was clear that some of the best and most desirable cars in the world were being shipped to Russia. Most were coming from Japan and, if Portunoff was taking the usual ten percent broker's fee, St. Scot realized that the Russian was a very rich man.

"Most of these cars are still in Japan. I haven't delivered them yet. For my comrades, just knowing they own such wonderful vehicles is sometimes enough. It gives them bragging rights," said Portunoff.

St. Scot recognized one of the cars on the list was the pre-war Mercedes-Benz SSKL supercharged sports car that he'd worked on when it was owned by Filby, ten years earlier.

"This car," said St. Scot. "The Mercedes. I worked on it for Filby. The rear fender was creased when the car was being shipped back from a car show and Terry asked me to rework the piece to repair it."

Portunoff let out a low whistle. "An SSKL? One of the most beautiful sports cars ever! And your marks are on the fender?"

"Yes, right on the inside edge of one of the rear fenders. You can't see them, but I know where to look or feel for them, so I know they're there," said St. Scot, nodding.

Portunoff checked some of the papers he had brought with him. "That car was sold to a Japanese collector when the market and Japan's economy was strong," Portunoff said, checking some more paperwork. "Things have changed for its owner and his people came to me and offered to let me sell it. I am acting as a broker for the Japanese owner, in this case, but also as a buyer's agent for my comrades in Russia." Portunoff looked pleased with the arrangement. "The price to my Russian friend was well over four million dollars, which represented a loss to the Japanese of just over one and a half million dollars from when he bought the car a few years ago," Portunoff explained to St. Scot. "At least half of the cars that I am selling into Russia have come through deals that originally involved Terrance Filby," added the Russian. He looked thoughtful and then made a decision. "Simon, I'd like you to fly to Tokyo and meet with someone who will take you to look at this Mercedes. I want you to run your finger along the fender, and whatever else you need to do, to see if your secret marks are there."

St. Scot's long flight to Tokyo's Narita airport landed exactly on time. He had been to Japan a half a dozen times before, most recently for the Tokyo Motor Show. He had always flown business class at the expense of one of the car companies. This time he flew coach. Although Portunoff had told him to fly to Tokyo, and St. Scot assumed that the Russian would eventually reimburse him, he actually hadn't come right out and said so. It seemed safer to fly like a commoner.

The food in steerage class was not quite what St. Scot had experienced on his previous trips to Japan. In business class the food is tailored to western tastes, but in the back of the airplane on a flight to Japan it followed a more traditional direction: seaweed and some sort of dried cuttlefish, served as a snack. Predictably, the main course was fish, expertly steamed and served over rice, along with lightly steamed vegetables. The Japanese don't do desserts very well and St. Scot skipped the blob of sweetened rice that was offered. Instead, he sipped some warm sake and tried to get some rest.

It was shocking how tightly packed together the seats were in the back of the bus. Maybe the airline reasoned that Japanese people aren't as tall as Americans are and don't need the legroom. Fortunately, the aircraft was only half-full and St. Scot was able to stretch across three middle seats and get some sleep during the flight. The fact that it made a troop of Japanese schoolgirls who were seated nearby giggle was an added bonus.

St. Scot liked Japan. He liked the people, with their formal politeness and fanatical dedication to service. He liked the food, especially the exotic combinations of flavors of delicacies like eel, squid and octopus and even dried cuttlefish. Most of all, St. Scot enjoyed walking around a city like Tokyo, traveling through its complex subway system, towering over the average Japanese citizen and watching all of the millions of workers on their way to and from their jobs. As much as he tried not to, it was hard not to compare the people of every major metropolitan area to ants in a colony. All of their scurrying had always made him appreciate his own job and life as a journalist and how far removed from normal that it had been. He knew deep down he had Terrance Filby to thank for pulling him out of obscurity into the glamour of automotive journalism, the same Terrance Filby who now hated his guts. Was it possible that Filby was the mastermind behind of all of his woes?

On all of his previous trips to Japan, St. Scot had been the guest of one of the Japanese car companies and they had picked him up, shuttled him around and pampered him in the way that only the Japanese can. This time he figured he would be on his own, so he was surprised when he came out of the immigration area and into the brightly-lit main terminal to see a white sign with his name being held by a small, slim Japanese woman. He walked up and introduced himself. She was Tamara Itagaki, a Japanese-American with a degree from UC Berkley who said that she ran Vladimir Portunoff's Asian interests. St. Scot didn't know that Portunoff had Asian interests, but then two nights ago he hadn't expected to be now standing in Tokyo's Narita Airport.

Itagaki led St. Scot to her right-hand drive C-Class Mercedes-Benz sedan. She took him straight to his downtown Tokyo hotel, the Otami, and left him there with a warm smile and a promise to return in the early evening. After dinner, she planned to take him to Portunoff's warehouse so they could look at the car that was awaiting shipment. St. Scot, jet-lagged from the long trip and thankful for his Western-style room, showered and put his head down on the pillow for a short nap. Three hours later he awoke. He dressed hurriedly in taupe wool slacks, a dark blue button-down shirt, maroon silk tie and a silk black blazer and he headed downstairs, looking forward to meeting the attractive Miss Itagaki for dinner.

Tamara Itagaki didn't disappoint. She had traded her somewhat austere business suit for a short and simple, but very effective, little black dress. Her long, straight hair, which had been pulled up severely when she met him at the airport, was now loose about her shoulders. She smiled at him warmly, with an added twinkle in her dark eyes and put her small hand in his as they walked together across the street to the restaurant that she had selected. The food was sushi, incredibly fresh and perfectly and traditionally seasoned with ginger root and wasabi. She let him order and soon they were eating sashimi-style yellow-fin tuna and shark and hand rolls of smoked eel and spicy salmon skin, washed down by glasses of very cold sake. If the food was memorable, the conversation was equally spicy.

St. Scot asked few questions as the soft-spoken woman recounted her personal history. She seemed to enjoy talking about herself, but did so in an understated way that her American visitor found captivating and charming.

"I was born right here in Tokyo. My father and mother were very traditional Japanese. Actually they still are," she said. "When I was three, my parents moved us to California, and that's where I grew up. We had relatives in the Bay Area so we moved there. I didn't know I had so much family! Do you have a large family Mr. Simon St. Scot?"

"No, not really. I am an only child. A couple of cousins, is all. Neither of my parents are still alive."

"That's too bad. Or maybe not. I am an only child too, but there was always someone around to watch me. I could never get away with anything! Anyway, I went to UC Berkley and studied computer science and got a degree. It was all right for a while, but making machines do what I wanted them to do wasn't nearly as much fun as making people do what I wanted them to do." She said this with a level stare straight into St. Scot's eyes.

The pause stretched for several seconds. "Um, how do you happen to work for Mr. Portunoff?" St. Scot finally asked.

Itagaki smiled. "Oh, it was really a whim. I answered an ad for a receptionist position. They wanted someone who spoke Japanese and my parents had insisted that I speak only Japanese to them at home. The job was at Vladimir's West Coast office."

St. Scot hadn't known Portunoff had a West Coast office.

"I think Vladimir saw in me a certain, um, moral flexibility that he recognizes in himself. You see, Mr. St. Scot, I am willing to do anything I need to in order to get what I want. People often underestimate me because I am a Japanese woman, but that's really just on the outside."

St. Scot was enjoying her outside, and she knew it.

"Inside I am really more like Donald Trump on steroids, which is probably why I get along with your friend Vladimir so well. He quickly promoted me ahead of the other people in his organization. When he needed someone to open his Japanese office, I found out about it early and pretty much cut off at the knees anyone else who might have been in line for the job."

St. Scot was impressed. She was witty, bright, extremely attractive and practically amoral; perfectly suited to moving ahead in the business world.

"The only thing I didn't count on, Mr. St. Scot, may I call you Simon? The only thing I didn't count on Simon was how boring it would be to live in Japan. For all of the talk about exotic Asian sexual practices, this place is pretty repressed."

St. Scot knew she was flirting with him, but assumed she was doing so just to keep in practice. He was old enough to be her, well, at least her older brother. She was never overt, but the seductive look in her eye kept him hanging on her every word, however, and made him think that she could be his if he played his cards right. He figured that was exactly the effect she wanted to have and she was obviously enjoying the confirmation that she hadn't lost a bit of her abilities while being cooped up with all of those stuffy Japanese suits.

They finished their dinner and the valet brought their car to the door of the restaurant. Itagaki drove and St. Scot was content to sit back and watch her handle the Mercedes as she sliced through Tokyo's busy streets. Even late into the evening, the traffic in Tokyo is terrible. For St. Scot it was a mystery why the Japanese had such a fondness for fast sports cars and rugged four-wheel drive sport utility vehicles, especially when heavy traffic meant that they could rarely drive over 35-mph, not to mention there's no suitable place to drive off-road. Itagaki's hands rested lightly on the wheel and she drove smoothly and without drama. St. Scot watched and admired her without feeling the need for much conversation.

After awhile they arrived at a low office building that was attached to a large warehouse. It was surrounded by a tall, steel fence with a guardhouse at an imposing but unmarked gate. The guard at the front gate obviously recognized Itagaki and didn't question her about the American in the car with her. They passed through the gate, parked the car and Itagaki opened the door to the office building, after punching in a security code. Leading him through the offices, they walked straight into the dimly lit warehouse. Itagaki threw a few switches and the mercury-vapor lights came on, illuminating row after row of classic cars. The effect was breathtaking and she knew this. Tossing her head back, she laughed.

"You should see how big your eyes are!" she said.

St. Scot stammered, "I had no idea that Vladimir was into this so deeply. This is incredible. There must be a quarter of a billion dollars worth of cars in this room."

She smiled and looked upward for an instant for a quick mental calculation. "Yes, about that, maybe more," she said quietly.

Taking his hand, she led St. Scot through the maze of cars. Here and there she would point out a Hispano-Suiza or an early Ferrari or a Delahaye that was particularly beautiful or curvaceous. She had exceptional taste in automobiles. For St. Scot it was sensory overload. Here were arguably some of the best cars in the world, worth a king's ransom. No, given the current state of royalty worldwide, worth several kings' ransoms. As Itagaki led him through the aisles he began to understand how heavily the Japanese had been into collecting.

Itagaki finally stopped in front of a huge, black, early 1930s Duesenberg Limousine. Taking both of his hands she stood on her toes to kiss St. Scot on his mouth. It was unexpected, but very pleasant. She smiled enigmatically and slowly walked around to the back of the huge pre-War car.

"Although this is not the most impressive or beautiful car here, it is my favorite of all of them," she said in a soft voice. "They say this car was used by Tallulah Bankhead in Hollywood." She paused, then continued. "They say it was the place she best enjoyed entertaining her many men friends, and even some of her female ones," she added softly. "I have always admired Miss Bankhead, and not just because Marlene Dietrich once said that she was the most immoral woman who ever lived."Tamara's voice took on a more direct tone. "I would really enjoy it, Mr. St. Scot, if you would join me in the back of this lovely automobile so that I can bring to life a fantasy of making love in the same place that she did."

With that, Itagaki shrugged out of her little black dress, confirming what St. Scot had suspected about what she wasn't wearing underneath, and opened the door to the Duesenberg. The subtle curve of her back matched the classic lines of the sublime cars around her. Her long black hair swished as she stepped up into the soft red heart of Tallulah Bankhead's automotive boudoir. Simon St. Scot had to join her. How could he resist the pull of history?

She was an aggressive but thoughtful lover, with an intense and almost frightening animal savagery, and she had brought along the condoms. The car rocked on its old springs to a rhythm that must have been familiar to it. Perhaps the ghost of Miss Bankhead was looking on with appreciation. It was an incredible experience and St. Scot felt as though he were being mauled by a tigress. He was in way over his head and loved every minute of it.

Later, lying sprawled across the rear compartment of the old car, and after his eyes had uncrossed and could focus again, St. Scot was amused to see that the windows of the old car had fogged up. He wondered how many times Miss Bankhead had fogged these very windows on sultry summer Hollywood nights. Itagaki lay curled up against him. Her eyes were closed and she was smiling happily.

"Thank you Mr. St. Scot. I am happy you seemed to enjoy my fantasy as much as I did."

St. Scot nodded sleepily. "Even though I may now be crippled for life, I am happy and proud to have been a part of it," he said grandly.

After a companionable silence, they both got out of the car and found their clothing. "I suppose now you will want to look at the car in question," she said, business-like once more.

"I think Mr. Portunoff would prefer that I did, yes," answered St. Scot politely.

The large, white Mercedes-Benz sports car sat in the back part of the building, not far from the loading docks. With its long hood and gleaming, exposed, snake-like, nickel-plated exhaust pipes, the car was as imposing as St. Scot remembered it. The proportions of the car were exquisite and even with its great length, the tiny cockpit was a cramped fit for a racing driver and his riding mechanic.

St. Scot walked slowly around the car and admired its high wire-spoke wheels and curving lines. It certainly looked right; it was a racing car built for a different age, when real heroes raced on open unpaved roads to glory or death. All at once, St. Scot turned to Itagaki and gave her a long passionate kiss. He then walked to the down slope of the right-rear fender and reached under the car. The line of the fender bead felt smooth to his touch. To be sure, he checked again. None of his tiny secret marks were there.

CHAPTER 22

"I trust then that my Miss Itagaki took good care of you?" Vladimir Portunoff's voice crackled over the phone line.

"Um, well yes, yes she did," stammered St. Scot.

"Yes, I'm sure. She is an enthusiastic young woman and is quite bored by living in her homeland," said Vladimir succinctly. "So, now to business. While you've been in Japan, I've been setting into motion some other, shall we say, actions? I assumed that you would find that the Mercedes was a fake and I have delayed its sale. But, more importantly, we have to now make plans for how we will turn all of this to our own advantage."

A chill went down St. Scot's back. He *was* in over his head. He knew it when he saw the list of cars that Vladimir was dealing in. He knew it when he saw the warehouse full of cars in Japan. He definitely knew it when Miss Itagaki had shrugged out of her little black dress. Yet deep inside, a tiny flame was burning. Anger. He wanted someone to pay for what they had done to him.

"Vladimir, I…" St. Scot began.

"Don't worry Simon, you won't have to do anything. Well, not so very much anyway. I am taking care of all. I have the necessary, um, skills and people to make all of this happen." Portunoff was very reassuring.

"No, Vladimir. I wanted to say that, well, I want to be there when you get the person who did this to me…" said St. Scot.

"Really? Ah, vengeance is mine and all of that! Okay, Mr. Automotive Journalist, I'll see if I can make that happen. For now there is work to be done."

The next day an unmarked car transporter pulled up in front of the farm. St. Scot was in the barn fighting against jetlag and came out when he heard the truck slow for the turn onto his driveway. The driver of the transport told St. Scot that he had instructions to deliver the car inside to the farm. Together, they opened the back door of the trailer and St. Scot whistled involuntarily. Sitting inside, carefully strapped into place, was Portunoff's red Allard. After helping the man unload the car, St. Scot locked it into the barn and went back up to the house to make a phone call. Again Portunoff caught the phone between its first and second rings.

"Ah yes, Simon, I was expecting your call. I trust my Allard got there safely then?"

St. Scot stammered that it had just arrived. "But how did you get it back…" he started to ask.

Portunoff interrupted him. "Don't worry about that now. I will tell you when I see you. In the meanwhile, could you please make for me a new fender for the Allard to replace the missing one?" asked the Russian.

St. Scot agreed and Portunoff rang off before St. Scot was able to ask any more questions.

St. Scot went to the barn and started to work on the fender immediately. By lunchtime he had removed the other fender and had used it to lay out a pattern. He then went up to the farmhouse for a bite: a bean sprout and smoked cheddar on sourdough bread sandwich with a glass of cold apple cider, and then returned to the shop. He liked to work with classical music in the background and the local public radio station was very accommodating.

As the fender progressed, St. Scot realized that his metalworking skills were improving. Some of the old craftsmen he had interviewed told him that would sometimes happen. You could spend years doing the same things over and over again, never getting any better, and never getting any worse. Then one day, out of the blue, you could suddenly bend metal into shapes like never before. It was as if you had suddenly leapt from a plateau and had reached a new level. St. Scot felt that way as his hands worked the metal of the Allard's fender. After a couple days work, the fender he had produced would be the equal of the other three on the sports car. Then it would need to be sent away to the paint-shop that Terrance Filby used, in order to precisely match the color on the car.

In the middle of the afternoon, he heard the crunch of gravel as a car pulled into the drive. Coming to the door of the workshop he saw a non-descript Ford Taurus parked by the house and Detective Linda Jameson walking toward the front door of the farmhouse. He called out and she turned and changed course, heading for the barn.

"Mr. St Scot," she began. "I've learned that you went out of the country without telling me that you were leaving."

"Ah, detective, well, I guess I forgot," he said.

"Forgot? Do you realize that as you are a material witness I could arrest you for flight?" she asked.

"No, I guess I just wasn't thinking. I'm sorry."

"What were you doing in Japan?" she asked.

"Just some consulting work for an car collector," he said. "You wanted to talk to me about something?" asked St. Scot, changing the subject. "Does it have to do with Bill Borgenson or with my firehouse?"

Detective Jameson said, "Yes, Mr. St. Scot. Both, actually. Short of any additional evidence, we will be finding that Mr. William Borgenson died of a self-inflicted gunshot wound. That is, unless you have anything else you want to tell me."

St. Scot hesitated. "Why did you ever think it was otherwise?" he asked.

Jameson looked annoyed. "We received an anonymous tip that somebody might have a reason to kill him. It took some time but that information finally led to a series of dead-ends."

"Just out of curiosity, Detective Jameson, did any of those tips point in the direction of me?"

She looked indecisive for a second and then made up her mind. "Yes, Mr. St. Scot, they did. You might already be aware of this, but you have some pretty nasty enemies."

"Which brings us to my firehouse," said St. Scot.

"Which brings us to your firehouse," she repeated.

"Listen, before we start on that, I was just going to make some fresh coffee, would you look to have some?" St. Scot asked.

"Decaf," she said.

As they entered the barn, Jameson's attention was immediately drawn to the airplane in the shadows. "You have a Gypsy Moth!" she exclaimed. Rushing over to it she ran her hand along its wooden propeller. All pretense of officialdom was gone. "Wherever did you get it?" she asked excitedly.

St. Scot told her the story of his father's pride and joy. After a few minutes of carefully examining the vintage aircraft she smiled at him. It was the first time he had seen her smile. He was somewhat taken aback by her transformation.

"In addition to sports cars, my dad loved airplanes. He had flown in the Korean War and never flew after that, but he would drag me to air shows all over the country," she said. After a pause she added, "For what it's worth Mr. St. Scot, I am really sorry about what happened to your firehouse. You really had some beautiful cars and it must really hurt."

"You like cars then?" asked St. Scot.

She nodded. "We went to car shows, too, and to the occasional Concours. It's funny though, as much as my dad pushed me to sports cars, I seem to be drawn more toward the big luxury cars of the thirties. My favorites have always been Duesenbergs…"

St. Scot felt his hair stand on end as his most recent experience with a Duesenberg came flooding back. For an instant he wondered if somehow she knew more about his Tokyo trip than she was letting on, but she was still rhapsodizing about her favorite car.

"There is just something about all that power and speed, yet the almost sinful levels of luxury and comfort. You can almost sense what it would be like to be a movie star in the thirties with a car like that. Can you imagine? They just don't make cars like that today," she said wistfully.

He nodded. Yes, he could imagine.

"And what's this?" she asked, pointing to the partially disassembled Allard. "If I am not mistakened, that's an Allard." She paused and looked at St. Scot. "Didn't you say an Allard was missing from the cars in your warehouse?"

St. Scot felt trapped. Should he lie to the police detective? If he told the truth it would just open a can of worms. She was waiting for an answer. "Well, yes. I mean yes an Allard was missing, but this one belongs to a friend of mine and it needed some work so he sent it over." *Did she buy it?*

"I see," she said.

She wasn't buying a word of it and what they both knew was a lie brought her back to being a cop.

"Your firehouse, as you know, was a case of arson," Jameson began. "It's still under investigation, but as we are understaffed, not much progress has been made. I would think the insurance companies will eventually settle, but there just isn't much that we can do until we get some better leads."

St. Scot poured the coffee and added some cream from an ancient refrigerator that sat humming in the corner of the workshop.

"So, Detective Jameson. By the way, may I call you Linda? What is it that you came all the way out here to tell me?" St. Scot asked.

She smiled again and took a sip of coffee. "Look Simon, you seem like a nice-enough guy. Let me level with you. My police instincts tell me you are into something pretty bad and that you need help. My instincts as a woman, which by the way have never failed me, tell me that you are probably a pretty good person, even if you don't exactly always tell all of the truth. If you tell me what the real story is, we can go after whoever is doing this. I won't lie to you, it would be a real feather in my cap in the department, too, if I could solve this."

St. Scot smiled back at her. "Detective. Linda. I don't know exactly what to say. I have had some bad luck, haven't I? I need to think things through a bit and maybe then we can talk again?"

She rose and started toward the door. "That's fine, Mr. St. Scot. You have my number and can reach me."

The next day, a dark green Bentley Turbo R pulled up to St. Scot's farmhouse. Inside, Vladimir Portunoff was driving while a large heavyset man sat next to him. Portunoff greeted St. Scot warmly and introduced the other man as David, his bodyguard. The large man's hand dwarfed St. Scot's own. *It was clear that Portunoff hadn't hired him just for his intellect or his conversational skills.* Portunoff dismissed the bodyguard to the front porch of the old farmhouse and pulled up a chair to the kitchen table. He opened his leather briefcase and pulled out a series of documents. Glancing at them, St. Scot could see that some were written in English while others were in Japanese and Russian. Vladimir looked over them briefly and then smiled at St. Scot.

"First things first, Simon. How is my Allard?" the Russian asked.

St. Scot smiled. "I have the fender almost finished and it is coming out really well. It just needs a bit more shaping and then you need to send it to the paint shop and then it can be put back onto the car. I am sure that Mort Welsh can tell you what paint code it should…" St. Scot stopped in mid sentence.

Of course! The Allard, the original one that St. Scot had worked on had been a very specific color of red. It was a special mixture that was specified by Terrance Filby. They had joked about it being the color of Barbara's favorite lipstick. St. Scot was sure of it: *The fake car in St. Scot's barn was exactly that same color.*

Vladimir looked at him quietly. "You are thinking of the paint colors and how hard they would be to match?" said Portunoff.

St. Scot nodded his head. "Yes, I just now thought of that, but what does it mean?"

Portunoff looked at St. Scot sadly. "It means, my dear friend, that your colleagues Mr. Filby, Mr. Welsh, and probably Mr. Marshfield and even that clown Ivan Blinsky are into this up to their necks."

"How did it all work?" asked St. Scot.

"The scam was always pretty straightforward, but it required a lot of planning and organization. As you know, your good friend Terrance Filby purchased a large number of classic formula and sports racing cars during the seventies and early eighties when the prices were fairly low."

St. Scot knew that the only people buying old race cars in those days were eccentric collectors who liked to show them or sometimes race them in old car events. It was hard to think of them as investments back in those naïve days when nobody really wanted a beat-up old aluminum-bodied Ferrari racing car, for example. With a booming economy in the late eighties, however, a whole group of new people suddenly decided that owning a classic car was the thing to do. Some say the mania was sparked by a single collector who suddenly decided he had to have one certain car no matter what the price. Others figured there was just too much money in the hands of middle-aged men who were tired of playing golf. In any case, this set the stage for a frenzy of buying and selling of anything old and automotive. Ferraris that were bought and sold for $30,000 one month were bringing almost a million dollars three months later. Speculators were buying old cars as fast as they could and making fantastic profits in less than six months time. These people didn't actually buy the cars to drive or because they were beautiful to look at. They were in it for the money. St. Scot remembered those times well, mostly because it was when he was struck by the harsh realization that many of the classic racing cars of his dreams would forever be beyond his means.

"So when the market exploded, Mr. Filby already had a treasure trove of desirable old racing cars and speculators came to him offering fantastic sums of money for his cars," Portunoff continued. "You probably know that this was when he hired Mort Welsh so that the two of them could make even more money." Portunoff sighed. "At some point, shortly after Welsh started working for Filby, your services were no longer required as a metal fabricator, and the process of building fakes began. In fact, it may have been Welsh who first brought the scheme to Filby."

St. Scot couldn't help feeling a bit disappointed when he heard that Filby hadn't considered him to be his partner in crime. Would St. Scot have played along and become a rich man alongside his boss and mentor? He wasn't sure that he could answer that.

Portunoff continued. "Filby, because of his status as the patriarch of automotive journalism, had a reputation that was unassailable. Filby had you and Borgenson write up those lavish histories on each of his cars to convince the world of their veracity. Your histories would be created while looking at and researching the real car and then used as a guide to create perfect copies. Most of the deals in those days were done one-on-one and many of the cars went to Japan, purchased sight unseen by the rich Japanese buyers. Your Terrance Filby got to keep his treasured real cars while selling the fakes off as the originals for millions of dollars. He didn't just sell the fakes, of course, and the collection the public knew about grew smaller as some of the second-tier, less valuable, cars were also sold to collectors in the Orient." Portunoff took a deep breathe. "I estimate that Filby and Welsh probably made nine or ten individual fake cars, including my Allard, which I think we both agree would have been pretty easy to recreate. I actually think the Allard was in fact their first try at counterfeiting," he said.

"They could have gone on indefinitely if the Japanese economy hadn't crumbled. Filby was contacted by a group of Japanese collectors who had purchased cars from him. They needed to sell their cars and wanted him to help broker the deals with their new friends, the Russians. Filby and Welsh obviously saw this as a golden opportunity. The cars that were already fakes they could sell again as originals, the provenance impeccably proven by the leather-bound histories and the connection to known Japanese collectors. Other cars from the Japanese collectors that they were offered could be duplicated if they were valuable enough, using original spare parts that Filby had been collecting to aid in the deception," said Portunoff. "But they needed a front guy in Russia and Filby had contacted me to help broker the sales. Your good buddy neglected to tell me that some of the cars were counterfeit. The fake cars were sold to the Russian buyers through my Japanese operation that you visited." Portunoff added. "Meanwhile, the originals could be spirited away back to Filby's private collection. Filby and Welsh had set up a shop in Korea in an out-of-the-way spot outside of Seoul and had little trouble finding skilled Korean craftsmen to work on counterfeiting the cars," said Portunoff. "Filby was quite obsessed with owning as many exquisite originals as possible, even if he and Mort Welsh were the only ones who could ever see them. Many of the cars that Filby sold from Japan were the real thing. They only counterfeited the most unusual and valuable examples. I figure they made another four or five cars in their secret Korean workshops."

St. Scot recognized it as a scam that was lifted from the art world, now applied to classic cars of the first order. It was impressive, but St. Scot couldn't figure out what it had to do with him and his job as a magazine editor. He asked Portunoff and the Russian hesitated before explaining further.

"This part isn't as clear as the first part," said the Russian slowly. "But this is where our Mr. Marshfield comes into the picture. It seems when the Fishers were selling their beloved magazine, your Mr. Terrance Filby was one of the primary bidders. He and Bill Borgenson had put together a group of investors to buy the magazine and run it in their own way. Except when WPI entered the bidding it quickly outbid what good old Terrance could afford." Portunoff said.

"By the time he was able to raise additional funds, the Fishers had already signed a contract with WPI and no matter how angry Filby was, there wasn't much he could do about it."

St. Scot imagined that Filby must have been well and truly pissed at missing a chance to own the magazine.

"But here is where it gets interesting," said Portunoff, leaning forward. "Winston Marshfield was the guy at WPI who put the deal together with the Fishers, effectively freezing out Filby. As a member of the board of WPI, I can tell you we were all pretty impressed with our Mr. Marshfield. But from the information I have just been gathering, it appears Winston Marshfield is what we would have called in my old days a double agent."

The former KGB agent looked positively wistful for the old days for a few seconds.

"He began working with your Mr. Filby and together they devised a plan to run the magazine into the ground so that Filby could buy it cheaply from WPI once everything had gone to pot. But Filby had to get fired first to make it all work out and Bill Borgenson apparently decided to go along with him in the scheme. Marshfield brought in Ivan Blinsky to run the place, almost a guarantee of failure..." said Portunoff smiling.

St. Scot sat thinking for a few seconds. "What does Marshfield hope to gain from all of this?" he asked the Russian.

"Winston apparently wants to have his own publishing empire and is willing to build it out of the magazines he wrecks for WPI. As a board member I can tell you I am unhappy. As a comrade to several of the powerful Russians who own WPI, I can tell you that we will not let this happen," said Portunoff with great intensity.

"But how does all of this involve me?" asked St. Scot.

Portunoff leaned back and chuckled. "Oh, you are just a pawn. Marshfield thought that they could get you to play along, but Filby told them it wouldn't work, that you are too much of a, how do you say, a Boy Scout. But they tried and then they threatened you and when you didn't get the hint they realized that getting the honor-bound Mr. St. Scot out of the way was going to be in everyone's interest."

Portunoff seemed to think this was all very funny.

"Normally, they would have just killed you and made it look like suicide like they did with Borgenson." the Russian explained. "Borgenson had discovered Filby's car scheme earlier and had been happy to produce the leather bound provenance books for a piece of the action. But he was being cut out by Filby and so he called you to join him in a blackmail deal," Portunoff continued. "He wanted to blackmail Filby over the cars and Marshfield over the WPI deal. Clearly, one of them didn't think much of his blackmailing scheme, and anyway, Marshfield needed the hold of the fake car scam to lord over Filby's head. Borgenson was just stupid and greedy."

"So Borgenson knew? About the fake cars I mean?" asked St. Scot.

Portunoff gave him a pitying look. "Your faith in the goodness of humanity is touching. Misplaced, but touching. They probably should have eliminated you, too, in case you figured it out. Instead they simply took away any evidence that you might have, as well as that life you loved so much. If I hadn't bumped that other car with my Allard at Lime Rock and sent it to you to be fixed, you would have been none the wiser and might have stayed and worked for Blinsky," said Portunoff.

St. Scot thought over all that Portunoff had said. *It was incredible.* St. Scot tried to think of any reason that Portunoff would have to lie to him. But Portunoff had explained it so matter-of-factly that it almost had to be true. His whole life ruined so that Terrance Filby could keep a king's ransom in classic cars and Winston Marshfield could own a publishing empire? Well, maybe it wasn't so crazy. In fact, the more he thought about it, the more sense it began to make. At least it was finally an explanation.

"How did you find out all of this information so quickly?" St. Scot asked of the Russian.

"I am pretty sure you don't want to know this." He paused. "It really comes down to knowing who to ask, what to ask and how to ask them..." Portunoff said flatly.

St. Scot shuddered. "All I wanted to do was drive cars and write about them," he moaned. "I write for an entertainment magazine. I don't want to be involved in the KGB and the Russian Mafia and whatever else is going on."

Portunoff looked at him sadly for a moment. "Yes, well you are involved, my friend, and so am I. So instead of complaining, let me tell you how we are going to change it all so the game works in our favor."

Chapter 23

St. Scot drove slowly passed the burned out fire station that had once been his home. The insurance company had done an efficient job boarding up all of the shattered windows and the charred doors. Soot covered the exterior walls and the building looked like it was hardly worth saving. Inside lay the charred remains of his whole life, grim reminders that the bad guys he was involved with played for keeps.

Portunoff's plan was audacious, and costly. But the Russian seemed to have no qualms about bankrolling the whole thing. Either he was stinking rich or he was playing with other people's money. St. Scot thought about the hundreds of millions of dollars worth of old cars in Portunoff's Japanese warehouse and decided not to ask the Russian how he was going to pay for the operation.

In the two days since their meeting in St. Scot's farmhouse, Vladimir had pulled together his formidable resources and had received permission to borrow ten of the fifteen cars he knew to be fakes. Eight of these had actually been stored in his Tokyo warehouse. The others would be made available. The owners of these treasures were men who worked entirely on personal contacts, and as Portunoff explained, "If I need to borrow their cars, they're willing to trust me."

Meanwhile, St. Scot had an ulterior motive to be in the city. Detective Jameson had agreed to go to lunch with him. He had called her and asked her, and, after a slight hesitation, had said yes. He wasn't sure if it was to further the case or because she was interested him, but he would take what he could get.

She picked the place. It was a Vietnamese restaurant on the other side of the airport. St. Scot arrived first at the uncrowded restaurant and got a table. Jameson arrived shortly after. She set her heavy handbag at her feet after sitting down.

"I'm so glad you could come," he said.

"I wasn't sure I could get away. I told you how busy we've been lately, what with firehouses burning down and such," she said.

"This is nice," he said looking around. "I've not been to this place before. Is the food good?"

"I like it," she said, "but then I've always been partial to Asian restaurants."

"The way you handled the restaurant choice makes me think you've been doing this all of your life," said St. Scot.

"What makes you think I haven't?" she replied a bit testily.

"Oh, nothing. What right do I have to think?" he said.

She laughed. "Peter Lorre in that scene in 'Casablanca,' right?"

He laughed too. "Yes, exactly right!"

"I love that movie. My father and I used to watch it every New Year's Eve when I was growing up."

"He must have been quite a guy," said St. Scot.

"Oh, he was the best! I was an only child. Mom couldn't have any more children after me. I think secretly he always wanted a boy, and I always tried really hard to be the best tomboy that I could be, to make up for it. My mom was very understanding. She still is. I talk with her at least once a week. She's in a nursing home in Florida."

This was almost like a date, or at least he thought so. He still wasn't sure how Jameson felt. She was wearing a gray blazer over a cream silk blouse and looked much more feminine than when he had seen her before. He wore a black blazer and no tie. Her green eyes sparkled. They didn't talk about arsonists or suicides.

When they were finished with lunch, they lingered in the parking lot. She had driven in her own car, a bright red Miata, not the official unmarked police car.

"Simon, this was fun," she said.

"Yes, maybe we can do it again, soon?" he asked.

"Well," she began.

"What is it?" he asked.

"Well, up until a short time ago you were a suspect in one of my investigations," she said. "I like to keep my business and personal lives separate, and you're making that difficult. I'd like to see you again. I'd like that very much. Only Simon, when it comes time for me to round up the usual suspects, you just make sure that you're not one of them." She made this last comment with a smile on her face, but there was an underlying message.

They shook hands politely and left. He figured he would count it as their first date. Aside from that last part, it was the most normal day that St. Scot had experienced in months. What a relief.

A week later, Portunoff arrived from London with his body-guard and met St. Scot at the Russian's downtown hotel. Portunoff embraced him warmly, looking like a cat who had just disposed of a canary.

"Ah my friend Simon," he said, "the game is in motion. I tell you, things could not be going more smoothly."

Portunoff had set up a meeting with Filby and had suggested that it take place at Filby's own home. On the way there he and St. Scot discussed what they needed to get out of Filby in order to make everything happen the way it should.

"He won't be happy to see you," said the Russian, "but I just want him to know that you and I are working closely together. Sort of rattle his cage, as you might say."

Portunoff had neglected to mention that St. Scot would be coming, so it was an angry Filby who came out of his front door to meet them as the Russian's Bentley pulled up to the house.

"What the hell is he doing here!" demanded Filby in an indignant voice. "I told that scum I never wanted to see his face around here again. As far as I'm concerned, Vladimir, you can just get back in that car and hit the road! As long as he's here you and I have nothing to discuss."

Portunoff cleared his throat and spoke quietly. "Terrance, do not be stupid. Mr. St. Scot is working for me now. As for nothing to discuss? Could we not even discuss my very beautiful Allard?"

Portunoff took his wire rim glasses off and slowly pulled out a soft cloth and began polishing the lenses – something

Heinrich Himmler used to do before condemning a man to Nazi torture.

Portunoff's quiet remarks had a remarkably calming effect on Filby. Filby motioned for the two men to come into his labyrinth of a house. They followed him to the sun porch and found seats.

"Terrance, let me be blunt," began Portunoff. "We know that you have a collection of extremely valuable classic cars, and that these cars are the originals and that you and Mort Welsh have fabricated fake cars and sold them while keeping the real ones."

Filby started to protest, but Portunoff cut him off with a wave of his hand.

"Don't bother, Terrance. If you want me to, I can give you a list of exactly which cars you faked, but we are all gentlemen here, so I know that just making the offer to do so will be enough to convince you that I know what you have been doing."

Filby said nothing.

"Terrance, it was okay for you to play your little game when you were dealing with the Japanese. They are a civilized people. But now you are dealing with Russians. My countrymen, many of whom are savages. They suspect everyone and trust no one. I know this because I am one of them." Portunoff paused for effect. "Terrance, if I could figure this out in such a short period of time, with the help of my good friend Simon here, how long do you think it will take others who are less, shall we say, charitable, to find this out? You are in grave danger, comrade, and you have placed me, and also our Mr. St. Scot, in equally great danger."

Filby sat motionless for more than a minute. Then quietly said, "What do you wish to do?"

Portunoff nodded. "Good," he said. "Terrance, I am bringing all of the fake cars together here, in a secret location. When I have them, we will swap them all for the real ones that you have and then destroy the copies. This must be done in case any of my comrades ever get wind that any of the copies ever existed. If they ever find out and even suspect that the fakes weren't destroyed, your wife would never find enough of you to bury."

Filby sat back in his chair. "Destroy them? Really? Maybe I could just keep the fakes and turn over the originals?"

Portunoff shook his head. "You just don't get it, Filby! Those cars are your death sentence. Either they go and you live, or they stay and you die. There is no other option."

St. Scot spoke for the first time. "I have just one question."

Filby looked at St. Scot. "Simon, are you going to ask, why did I do it? Why do you think? I did it for the money! Don't be so naïve. I loved those cars, but they were just getting to be worth so much, so here was my chance to keep them and also to cash in on the ridiculous prices. It was the best of both worlds, and nobody would have been the wiser, had you and Vladimir not stumbled onto it."

St. Scot shook his head. "No Terry, that wasn't what I wanted to know. I want to know how you could have destroyed the magazine you helped to build?"

Later, in the back seat of the big Bentley, Portunoff spoke to St. Scot, "You know your friend. Do you think he will play along?"

St. Scot thought for a moment. "I don't know. You say I know him, yet I never would have thought he could have been involved in this car scam. I never thought he would work with Marshfield the way he did. And I certainly never thought he could be a party to murder, if he was. If his relationship with Marshfield is as crooked as you say it is, I would guess that would be who he'll call next."

"Yes," replied the Russian. "A dangerous character, that Marshfield. One never knows what he will do next or why. I like to think we are a step or two ahead of him, but my old KGB sense tells me otherwise."

They rode in silence in the Bentley.

"Where are we going, by the way?" asked St. Scot as the driver turned onto a freeway heading away from Portunoff's hotel.

"I thought you might want to go and see some cars," Portunoff replied.

The car pulled through a high chain link fence and up to the front door of a large metal warehouse. An armed guard was standing outside looking formidable. Portunoff nodded to the guard who turned and unlocked the small entry door to the metal warehouse.

Inside the tall building, near its center, was a group of ten gleaming classic cars. At the center of the group, artfully lit by one of the building's mercury vapor lights, was a dramatic bright yellow racing car from the pre-World War I brass era. Any true automotive aficionado would immediately recognize it as a Stutz Bearcat. The Bearcat had always been one of St. Scot's favorites. Its high wheels, skimpy bodywork, cylindrical gas tank and monocle windshield all screamed sports car. Stutz automobiles were the work of Harry F. Stutz and the very first ones were entered in the earliest Indianapolis 500 races and finished admirably. The stunning success at the Indy race resulted in a slogan for the cars that they had "made good in a day." Their battles with the equally famous Mercers were the stuff of legends. "You couldn't do worser than to drive a Mercer," went the taunt from Stutz fans. "You must be nutz to drive a Stutz," came the reply from the Mercer camp. Very few of the big Stutz racing cars remained and the one before them was stunning.

The other cars were equally impressive. There was an Alfa Romeo 8C-2300 from the pre-war era, a Ferrari 125 Grand Premio from the early 1950s Grand Prix era, a sports-racing Delahaye, one of the kind so successful at the 24-Hour race at Le Mans just before and right after the war. Here was the huge white Mercedes-Benz SSKL that he had seen in Japan. The cars were magnificent, but he knew they weren't real. Each was an exact duplicate of a famous and nearly priceless racing car. No wonder Terrance Filby wanted to keep the originals all for himself. St. Scot had heard stories of art fanatics who would have a famous painting stolen and then display it in a private room, where only they could ever again see it. He had heard the stories of counterfeit masterworks being sold, while the original was safely stored away. For such people the possession of the item was more important than letting anyone in the world know that they had it. Filby had apparently simply applied the concept to the world of fine automobiles. He had all of the originals of these fabulous cars, but he couldn't ever show them or display them or even drive them. What a waste. He had to keep them locked away from the rest of the world or he would end up in prison, or worse.

St. Scot ran his hand slowly along the hood of a light blue Type 35 Bugatti racer from the late 1920s. It was exquisite, almost jewel-like in its petite size and intricate design. For a wild instant St. Scot thought it wasn't really so bad, what Filby and Mort Welsh were creating, if this was the result of their workmanship. But then, he wasn't a member of the Russian Mafia who had spent several million dollars to purchase an original and important racing car. All at once, St. Scot understood that Filby was in real danger. There was a good chance that, if Portunoff's comrades ever found out the truth, Terrance Filby and Mort Welsh would no longer be alive. No matter what he had done, was that what St. Scot wanted for his old friend and mentor?

"What's your plan?" asked St. Scot.

"Why, my plan is what it has been all along. To swap the fakes for the real cars, and then to quietly return them to my Russian comrades before they learn of the forgeries. It's the only way that you, me and your pal Filby will get out of this alive," the Russian said with a grin on his face. Portunoff seemed to find the whole situation a bit too funny, as far as St. Scot was concerned.

"What about the fakes?" St. Scot persisted.

"Ah yes. Well, as I said to Terrance, we will have to destroy them of course…It's a pity, isn't it? They really are beautiful," said Portunoff as he ran his hand along the curving flank of the pre-War Alfa Romeo.

"Won't Marshfield try to stop us?" asked St. Scot. "After all, they are the primary hold that he has over Terrance Filby."

Portunoff looked at him with approval. "Yes, my young protégé, we'll make a KGB agent out of you yet! Yes, Marshfield may be a problem. But for another reason too," the Russian said as they walked out of the building and nodded to the guard.

"Another reason?" asked St. Scot.

"Yes, there is the matter of Mr. Wilden and his Mysteria sports car," said Portunoff. "You know it, I believe?"

"Yes, it's a piece of rubbish. Nobody in their right mind would invest in it!"

"Ah, not so my naïve friend! Our Mr. Marshfield is heavily invested with his own and WPI's money."

"Why would he do such a thing?" asked St. Scot.

"Because Filby arranged it. Let me paint a picture. Suppose you had a great deal of money that was dirty, that you obtained illegally. To use this money in your legitimate enterprises you would need to launder it. Wilden's bogus sports car is the perfect vehicle for this money laundering. Marshfield invests in the project and then Wilden advertises heavily in the magazines that WPI owns. Filby set all this up and then sent his Boy Scout, Mr. Simon St. Scot, to write a story about the car to make it all seem legit."

St. Scot was aghast. Filby hadn't answered his question and now it was even worse than he thought.

"You seem shocked, Mr. Automotive Journalist," said Portunoff. "Don't be so surprised, it's more common than you might think. Oh, not the money laundering, but the trading of money for a favorable story. It was going on long before you were born and will still be around after both of us are gone," said the Russian. "They are just refining the system and getting better at it," he added.

St. Scot thought about Marshfield and that idiot Blinsky and he realized that what he was seeing here might indeed be the beginning of a terrible new dark age of automotive journalism. The emphasis lately had already gone away from the driving of the cars and focusing more on the lifestyle of the people who would buy them. Journalists were given the chance to sample a way of life far beyond their normal means and then write a story about how well the car in question would fit into that lifestyle. And if the car itself wasn't really that good? Well, if it fit so well with buyer demographics and expectations, why criticize it for a few minor dynamic faults? St. Scot had been fighting this attitude for years; now it appeared his fight was in vain. *The barbarians had overrun the gates.*

"Don't look so sad, comrade," said Portunoff. "We have a chance to put a stop to at least some of Marshfield's plans. Who knows? Maybe we can even find some revenge for you."

CHAPTER 24

For his next date with Detective Jameson, they went to a movie. They saw *Casablanca* on the big screen at a theater that specialized in classic movies. Shortly after the film began, Jameson reached over and took St. Scot's hand in her own. She snuggled down in her chair and he felt the warmth of her arm against his leg. Her handbag was between them and he shifted it, surprised at its heft.

"What are you carrying in here, bricks?" he whispered.

She smiled. "No, just my gun. We are required to carry it when we are in public and frankly it's a pain. It's a Glock. I'll show it to you sometime...."

Her hair smelled of citrus and next to his heavily armed date he felt truly relaxed. Together they watched Humphrey Bogart and Claude Rains fight the Nazis, while wooing the fair Ingrid Bergman.

"I never get tired of that movie," she said as they walked to her Miata. She had driven, after he had found a parking spot for his old pickup truck a block away from her apartment.

"It's one of the all time greats," he agreed. It was late and they drove in a companionable silence back to her place. He walked her to her door.

"Simon, I want to say something," she started.

"Yes, go on," he said, carefully.

"Simon, I like you. I like you a bunch. But I am also serious about my job," she said.

"I know that," he started.

"No, let me say this. If I thought for an instant that you had committed a crime, you wouldn't be here right now. Simon, I'm a cop. I'm not allowed to date criminals. It would just be so much easier if you would come clean. Tell me what you know and let me do my job. Really, I'm good at it, and I'm the one who gets to carry a gun and catch bad guys, remember?"

St. Scot reached out and hugged her. "I know," he said into her hair. "I just can't yet. Not until I know more about… well, how it's all going to work out."

She pulled away from him. "How it's all going to work out?" she said sharply. "Simon, I have a stake in this, too. My captain is really leaning on me to find the person who burned down your firehouse. This isn't a game! You have to tell me what you know, I just don't have any other leads! Why won't you trust me?"

He smiled at her and pulled her back to him. She resisted at first and then hugged him fiercely.

"I would invite you in, but it is very late and I do have an early meeting in the morning," she said primly.

He turned her head gently with his hand and pressed his lips against hers. It was a good first kiss. Not a great kiss, but the kind that promised greatness in the future. She turned and opened the door, and then turned back for another kiss. That one approached greatness, he thought to himself minutes later as he walked alone back to his pickup truck.

On one of his late afternoon visits to assess the progress on his firehouse, as he was getting out of his car, he was met by Allison Chalmers. She looked so mature and sophisticated he hardly recognized her. The young woman seemed a bit shy at first, while they walked together through the firehouse, looking at the progress the workmen were making.

"What is it, Ali? You seem like you want to tell me something," he asked.

"Oh Simon, you know how long I've had a crush on you. Don't deny it, I know you know."

St. Scot smiled at her and she took his hand.

"You have always been so careful around me and so proper, even when I really didn't want you to be..."

St. Scot was feeling uncomfortable. *Where was she going with this?*

"Well, although I'll always have feelings for you, kind of like an uncle, I have met someone..."

St. Scot felt a wave of relief. He managed to stammer, "Oh, that's super Ali, who is it?"

"Well, Simon, it's someone from work. We met at lunch one day and just sort of hit it off. I mean we haven't made any big plans or anything yet, but there is a connection, and we both feel it. I can't describe it, except to say that I feel really happy, do you know?"

"I'm really happy for you, Ali. You know I only want the best for you and Ronnie. What's your new beau's name?"

Allison giggled. "*Her* name is Amanda. She is as sweet as can be and she has already met Ronnie and thinks the world of him. Are you shocked, Simon?"

Allison's eyes were bright and she looked like a person in love. St. Scot turned and gave Allison a fatherly hug. "Shocked? No, more like envious. It sounds like you found someone special. I can't wait to meet her and I hope it works out for you." *Amanda? Who would have thought?*

"How are your parents handling it?" he asked.

"Well, at first dad like, freaked. Now they just tell me that it's only a phase I'm going through."

"Give them time, Allison."

"Oh, I know. But Simon, I feel sad for you. Still all alone? You need someone, too," Allison said.

Simon smiled. "Well, I'm working on that in my own way," he said.

"Is it a she?" she asked.

"It's a she," he answered.

"Is she nice?" she asked.

"She's a cop," he answered.

CHAPTER 25

He arrived at the German restaurant early and put his name in for a table. The early evening crowd was already hard at work, devouring schnitzel with spätzel and consuming large quantities of Warsteiner beer. As he waited for his table he saw Allison enter the restaurant with a short, well-rounded woman in a bright red coat. Allison spotted him and, grabbing the woman by the hand, pulled her over to him.

"Simon," she said while giving him a hug and a kiss on the cheek, "this is Amanda, who I told you about."

Amanda had a pleasant face and smiled at St. Scot as she held out her hand. "Delighted to meet you, Mr. St. Scot!" Her brown eyes were alive with seemingly perpetual amusement.

"Please, call me Simon, and I'll call you Amanda, if that's okay? I am very happy to meet you, too," said St. Scot.

The restaurant's hostess, a large woman who was a caricature of a German beer-maid, told them their table was ready.

"I can't imagine what's keeping Linda," said St. Scot. "She's usually very prompt."

Just as he said it, he saw Jameson come through the front door, dressed in a long coat and lugging her heavy purse. She saw him and her face lit up in a smile as she joined the group.

"Allison and Amanda, I'd like you to meet Linda Jameson," started St. Scot.

"I'm pleased to meet both of you and I'm starving, is our table ready yet?" she said all in one breath.

"Oh, but we've met before," said Allison. "You asked me some questions about the keys to Simon's firehouse after it burned down, remember?"

Jameson glanced at St. Scot and then replied, "Yes, of course you're right. I just didn't recognize you in this setting."

They found their table and ordered three beers and a diet soda for Allison. St. Scot took the liberty of ordering an appetizer of sausage and sauerkraut for the table, assuring them that they would love it.

As they studied their menus, Jameson asked Amanda, "So, tell me how you and Allison met?"

Amanda smiled and paused. The waitress brought the appetizers and took their dinner orders before she started. "Well, we met at work. I've been there three years as a paralegal, and Allison has just started as a receptionist. One day I went into the storage room to find some staples and, well, there she was putting away some new office supplies. Later that day, I was having trouble with the copy machine and suddenly there she was again, clearing the jam and helping me out," she said smiling at Allison. "Then, the next day, I saw her sitting on the front steps of the building eating her lunch and I sat down and joined her. I liked her company and asked if she wanted to see a movie that night and, well, here we are."

Allison looked at her new friend and blushed.

"What a nice story!" said Jameson, helping to cover up Allison's momentary embarrassment.

Allison asked Jameson, "So how about you two? Tell me Linda, was it love at first sight?"

Jameson laughed, "No, no, heavens no! I really didn't like Simon the first time I saw him. He seemed kind of smug and well, prissy. I actually thought he might be gay." All three women thought this was funny and laughed. St. Scot didn't quite see the humor.

"You didn't think he was just dreamy?" Allison asked, while winking at St. Scot.

"I guess he does sort of grow on you that way, but no, not when I first met him," she added with a smile.

"Allison tells me that you are in charge of the investigation into the fire at Simon's place. Do you have any leads?" asked Amanda.

Jameson scowled. "Not really. If Simon would just tell me what he knows and let me do my job, then maybe I could get somewhere."

The silence was awkward and went on for several long seconds.

"Ah, good, here comes our dinner," St. Scot finally said.

Behind the waitress bringing the platter with their dinners, St. Scot saw Ivan Blinsky, walking toward the table.

"Oh shit," St. Scot said.

The others turned just as the waitress arrived. Blinsky pushed past her and stood over St. Scot. "Look at this!" he said loudly. "An asshole, with his little bimbo friends!"

Blinsky must have been drunk. He was certainly acting erratically, even for Blinsky. St. Scot started to rise from the table when he felt Jameson's hand on his arm.

"Leave it, Simon," she said quietly.

Blinsky turned his attention to Jameson and started to say something, then looked at her more closely. "Hey," he said. "Hey, you're that cop who was asking me questions about the fire at his place. I didn't like your tone! What are you doing here, with him?" Blinsky swayed unsteadily. "You can do a lot better than him, baby!" he said with a leer.

"That's enough!" said St. Scot. "Why don't you just crawl back under whatever rock you came from and let us eat our dinner," said St. Scot. *Okay, it wasn't so original, but at least the message was clear.*

"You'd like that, wouldn't you Mr. Big Shot," said Blinsky. "And after all I did for you. All your staff ever says is Simon did this, and Simon did that. Well, I'm sick of it, and I'm sick of them, and as soon as I can, I'm going to can every-one and get a whole new staff. Running a magazine isn't so tough. You did it, and you're an asshole. Well, you're going to get yours, and when you do I want to be there to see it," Blin-sky said.

Jameson rose from her chair holding her handbag and said very quietly. "Mr. Blinsky. You are acting drunk and disorderly. If you don't leave immediately, I will arrest you. Furthermore, as you are clearly drunk, I will also arrest you should you decide to drive." She turned to the waitress, who was standing horrorstruck, watching the exchange while balancing the platter of food. "Miss, will you please arrange for a taxi for Mr. Blinsky."

Blinsky stared at Jameson for a few seconds. He glared at St. Scot and then spun around, catching the edge of the plat-ter of food in the hands of the hapless waitress. The platter tipped and, with a crash, their hearty German meals hit the floor. Almost before St. Scot had registered what had happened, Jameson had Blinsky's arm twisted behind him.

"Okay, pal," she said, "now you've gone too far! That was my dinner!"

"It was an accident," winced Blinsky. "I...I didn't mean to crash into her," he said almost whimpering.

"Then you won't mind explaining all of that to the manager and paying for the damages," she said. "Including our meals!" Jameson held Blinsky's arm firmly and marched him to the front of the restaurant while the other patrons looked on. An army of busboys came to clean up the spilled food. Presently, Jameson returned and took her seat, after helping Blinsky into the newly-arrived taxi.

"That was fun," said Amanda.

"What was that all about?" asked Allison, wide-eyed. Then to Jameson she said, "You were wonderful!"

Amanda looked jealous for an instant. So did St. Scot.

Jameson smiled. "It was nothing. It's what I do."

They tried to return to normal conversation and soon their replacement dinners arrived. The restaurant that St. Scot had chosen was well-known for its overly generous portions, and each of them needed a box for their leftovers. The dessert tray was impressive and St. Scot chose a Black Forest cake, sharing it with Jameson. Allison and Amanda each had their own apple strudel, and they all had decaf coffee.

After they left the restaurant and said goodbye to Allison and Amanda, St. Scot and Jameson stood in the parking lot next to her Miata and held each other in a loose embrace. He liked the warmth coming from her body. He liked it that they looked nearly eye to eye when they stood so close.

"That wasn't good," said Jameson.

"No, no it wasn't," agreed St. Scot.

"Are you ready to tell me what it's all about?" she asked.

"Linda, Blinsky is an idiot. He doesn't have the brains to do much beyond follow other people's instructions. I've known him a long time and what I am sure of is that he is little more than a pawn."

"Yes, I know that," said Jameson.

"The real power behind it all seems to be a guy called Marshfield. If Blinsky burned down my firehouse, then he did so because Marshfield ordered him to do it."

"And who is this Marshfield?"

"That's what I've been trying to find out. I think he's connected with the Russian mafia. I think he's really dangerous, but I have a friend who I'm working with. He's a Russian, too, an ex-KGB. He's got the right connections to figure out what's going on."

Jameson leaned in and gave St. Scot a long powerful kiss. "Do you know what I think, Simon? I think you are in way over your head and if you don't do something to let me help you soon, somebody's going to get hurt."

He wanted to protest, but she turned and slid into her Miata and drove off into the night.

CHAPTER 26

The sunlight streamed through the open door to the barn. They had pumped up a flat tire, and then rolled the Gypsy Moth out from where it had been stored. Jameson had driven out early in the morning in her Miata and together, she and St. Scot were carefully unwrapping the plastic coverings and tarps from the fabric wings and fuselage of the biplane. There had been a chill in the air earlier in the morning, but now the sun was warming the day nicely.

"I can't believe you grew up with this. It must have been fantastic," Jameson said, as she pulled a piece of plastic off of the engine cowling.

"I guess I never thought of it that way. Anyway, back then, this was just an old airplane and cars like my dad's Porsche 356 were just old sports cars. They weren't considered as objects d'art the way they are today," said St. Scot, working to remove a cover from one of the lower wings of the airplane.

She smiled at him and continued pulling off the plastic sheets.

"What's it like to fly in a Gypsy Moth?" she asked.

"It isn't really like flying, in the modern sense. You've flown in small planes and commuter planes and all, right?"

"Sure," she nodded.

"The Moth isn't like that. It shakes and vibrates and is noisy and the wind blows in your face and every little puff pushes you around. You can smell fresh cut grass and feel the air currents rising off of a field of corn," St. Scot said.

She was quiet for a few minutes and then said, "Sounds wonderful. Will you show me sometime?"

"Sure. You'll love it," he said.

"Yes. Yes, I'm sure I will"

"What made you want to be a cop?" St. Scot asked —a question he'd been wondering about for awhile.

"I didn't want to be a cop," Jameson answered. "I wanted to be a lawyer, but I ran out of money when my dad died and my mom went into the nursing home," she said. "Being a cop seemed to be a way to help people, and get some background, while I saved enough to go to law school."

"How long will that be?" he asked.

"About another year or so. Turns out I'm pretty good at being a cop and made detective in near record time…"

The first bullet struck the support between the upper and lower wings, just inches from St. Scot's head. The wooded spar shattered under the impact. The second bullet plowed into the wing, exactly where St. Scot had been standing an instant earlier, before Jameson shoved him aside.

"Get down!" she screamed as she hit the concrete floor and rolled behind the English Wheel, her pistol already out of the holster at the small of her back, coming around to return fire.

St. Scot scrambled to the other side of the open doorway, behind a workbench as Jameson fired two rounds through the open door toward the farmhouse.

"Are you okay?" Jameson called over to him.

"Yes, fine, are you?"

"Yep. Can you see from there how many of them there are?" she asked.

St. Scot peered around the edge of the workbench and a bullet ricocheted off the concrete floor.

"Is there a phone out here?" Jameson asked, in a voice that seemed unusually calm to St. Scot.

"Yes, there is, but it's over near the door, on my side," said St. Scot.

"I see," she said. "If I draw his fire and cover you, do you think you can reach the phone, and still be in a safe place?"

"I can try," he said.

"Good. Ready? Now!"

Jameson stood and turned facing the open door with both hands on her pistol. She fired three shots as St. Scot jumped and ran across the sniper's field of fire to the phone. He heard two shots from outside and turned to see Jameson spinning backward by the impact of a bullet. Her pistol clattered across the floor and landed by his feet. He picked it up and fired twice into the yard between the barn and house. One of his shots hit the windshield of Jameson's Miata, the other slammed into the door frame of the farmhouse. St. Scot had never been a very good shot. He grabbed the phone and dialed 911.

"A police officer has been shot, there is someone still shooting at us! We need an ambulance and help!" St. Scot screamed the address to the 911 operator and then dropped the phone. Outside, he could hear a vehicle starting out by the main road and, looking out the door, saw a black Chevrolet Suburban driving

quickly away. Seconds later, a red Dodge pickup truck bar-
reled down the road after it.

St. Scot grabbed the first aid kit he kept next to the phone
and rushed across the cement floor to Detective Jameson. She
had been hit in the neck. There was already a pool of dark
red blood on the ground and more was flowing freely from
her wound. From the kit he grabbed some gauze pads and
applied direct pressure to the bleeding gunshot wound. Her
eyes fluttered open.

"Simon," she gasped. "Simon, it's bad. Help me."

Her eyes closed and her breathing became more shallow. He
held pressure with one hand and stroked her hair with the
other, while tears ran down his face.

The ambulance arrived just ahead of the first police car. It
roared up the driveway and St. Scot called for help from inside the barn. Two young cops walked up carefully with their
guns in their hands and St. Scot very deliberately pointed to
Jameson's gun, lying next to the pool of her blood.

"Sir, please stand away from the gun and against the
workbench. I need to search you to make sure that you aren't
armed," one said, while the other watched nervously. The
paramedic behind them was a woman, who gently pushed
St. Scot aside and took over care of his patient.

Soon, the medics loaded Jameson into the ambulance and
it left with its siren wailing. St. Scot wanted to follow it to
the hospital, but the cops wanted to wait until their sergeant
arrived to take over the scene. After an agonizing half an hour
the sergeant finally arrived.

"Are you the one who called 911?" he asked St. Scot.

"Yes, after Linda, after the detective was shot, I managed to get a call to 911 and then, whoever it was that was shooting at us, left in a black Chevrolet Suburban," St. Scot replied. "Then a red Dodge pickup went by too. Listen, couldn't we do this at the hospital? I'm really worried about her," he added.

The sergeant checked with his superiors and it was agreed that St. Scot could be taken to the hospital by the patrolmen. St. Scot washed Linda's blood from his hands and arms and got into the back of the patrol car. He watched the police stretched crime scene tape around his side yard, between the farmhouse and the barn.

At the hospital, he was ushered into a waiting room. Nobody would tell him anything about Jameson. He wasn't family. He had no status that would require them to give him information. There were protocols to be followed. After an eternity, a large black man entered the waiting room and walked up to him.

"Are you Mr. St. Scot?" he asked politely.

"Yes, I'm Simon St. Scot," he said, offering his hand.

"I'm Captain Saunders. Detective Jameson works for me. I wonder if I might ask you a few questions. We can go in here," he said, pointing to a door at the end of the waiting room. "Listen, I need coffee, do you want anything?"

St. Scot asked for a coffee and then joined Captain Saunders in a small conference room. They sat at opposite sides of the table.

"I just have a few questions," said Saunders.

"First, could you tell me how she is?" St. Scot interrupted.

"Oh, of course. How thoughtless of me. She has a bullet wound in the neck, as you know. It just nicked the outer jugular vein, which is why there was so much blood. They tell me that your quick first aid probably saved her life, and for that I am grateful. She's in surgery now, to repair the vein. She did lose lots of blood, which has everyone worried, but her prognosis is excellent."

St. Scot slumped in his chair. It was as if all of the air had been let out of him. "Thank you," he said quietly.

"I'm glad to see you're so relieved, Mr. St. Scot. Now, if you please, could you tell me what happened? First of all, what was my detective doing at your house on her day off?"

Shit. How was he going to answer the captain's questions without getting Linda into trouble. "She came to talk about the arson at my firehouse," he said finally.

"Uh huh," said Saunders. "And at what time did she arrive?" he asked.

"I'm not sure," said St. Scot. "Maybe an hour or so before the shooting started."

"Can you tell me what happened?"

St. Scot explained the scene as best he could. In his mind all he could see was Jameson spinning around as the bullet struck her, and his voice caught as he told the story to the captain.

"Easy, Mr. St. Scot. Remember, she'll be okay," the captain said kindly, and paused. He then leaned across the table and asked pointedly, "Do you have any idea who might be wanting to kill you?"

Do you want a list? St. Scot thought to himself. Instead, he said "No, nobody."

Saunders looked at St. Scot. "Thank you Mr. St. Scot. I know that you are lying to me, and frankly, I can't wait to hear Detective Jameson's side of this whole thing. Meanwhile, stay in here as long as you wish, and let us know when you want to go home. A patrolman will give you a ride."

St. Scot sat in the waiting room until after midnight, well past the end of Jameson's surgery and after the nursing shifts had changed. They wouldn't tell him much, except that she was in intensive care in guarded condition. Exhausted, he finally asked the receptionist to call a taxi for him. It was a long ride home.

CHAPTER 27

It had begun to rain sometime after he arrived home from the hospital—a cold, dreary, rain that looked like it would stay for a while. As exhausted as he was, St. Scot slept little. His mind kept going back and forth between the events of the past weeks, and then to the shooting. *Marshfield was going to pay for this.* He was sure that was who was behind it. He was then struck by a thought. *Portunoff!* If both he and Portunoff were out of the way, Marshfield would be free to continue his plans to steal a publishing empire. He needed to contact Portunoff and warn him right away that his life was in danger! Quickly calling the hotel where Portunoff was staying, the operator answered and told him she would put him through. St. Scot was relieved to hear the Russian's voice, booming across the phone line.

"Vladimir, I'm glad you're safe. Something has happened," St. Scot began.

"Yes, I know Simon. Nasty business. I'm sorry my men didn't get to you to help you out. At least the girl will be okay, is that not so?" said Portunoff.

"Your men? They were there? What do you mean your men? How do you know about what happened, Vladimir?" St. Scot demanded angrily.

"I've had people watching you for some time now. I had a feeling that Marshfield might try something, and I wanted to make sure that you were safe. I'm just sorry that your friend got hurt. I take full responsibility. My men saw the shooter arrive, but just didn't react quickly enough. By the time they got into position to take him out, you apparently scared him away with your deadly accurate aim." St. Scot could almost hear him chuckle over the phone. "They chased him after he left, but he got away..."

"If you've been watching me then you know about Linda and me. You know who she is, I mean," St. Scot said cautiously.

"That she is a police detective? Yes, I know that. I also know you. You like to have all of the answers. I was certain you weren't going to tell her anything, not until you had it all figured out," said Portunoff. "She is a lovely young woman," he added.

"Vladimir, we have to do something. If Marshfield gets you and me, then he can continue his game with Terrance Filby and nobody will be the wiser!" said St. Scot.

"Just so, Mr. Junior KGB Agent," came the reply over the phone. "On the other hand, if we strike first, when he doesn't expect it, then we have a good chance of being the winners," said Portunoff.

"A good chance? How good?" asked St. Scot.

Portunoff laughed. "Oh, better than even, I should say. Probably better than the chances of you getting to drive at next year's race at Le Mans. What are you worried about? Nobody gets to live forever."

"After what he did to Linda, I don't need to live forever, just long enough to get Marshfield," said St. Scot.

"Ah, so now we have to avenge the injury to our fair maiden, in addition to the revenge we are owed for wrecking your life?" Portunoff said.

"Cut it out, okay? Just tell me what I need to do," said St. Scot.

"I need to make a few more preparations and get one more piece of information. I'll tell you what," said Portunoff, "meet me at one o'clock sharp at the place where we are keeping the fake cars, the warehouse. Do you remember how to get there?"

"Okay, I know where it is. I'll be there," said St. Scot.

When St. Scot's old pickup truck turned the corner into the warehouse parking lot, he saw the crumpled form of the security guard lying by the open doorway. Smoke was pouring from inside the building that held the fake cars. St. Scot rushed to the door, stepped over the fallen guard and peered into the building. Inside he saw a huge fire already blazing at the center of the warehouse. All of the cars were on fire and the flames were so intense it was impossible to make out the individual cars. The heat forced St. Scot away from the door. Just as he was retreating, the guard on the ground moaned. St. Scot quickly grabbed the man's collar and began pulling him across the wet lawn and gravel driveway, toward his truck, safely away from the burning building. When they reached the truck, St. Scot pulled out his cell phone and dialed for help. He then turned and ran back to the warehouse to see what he could save, but the blazing inferno was too intense and he retreated once again back to his truck.

The whole building was now fully involved in the blaze. Flames were licking along the roof and the front wall was beginning to buckle from the heat. The guard at his feet was beginning to regain consciousness and St. Scot knelt next to him and asked him what had happened. A large bruise was evident on the man's wet forehead. His hair was plastered to his head and he was still groggy.

The guard looked at St. Scot and, speaking weakly, said, "I don't know. A well-dressed man approached me, asking for directions. Then something hit me and I went down. Then he hit me again and the next thing I knew I woke up here."

The man's eyes turned to the building engulfed by the flames. "Oh God, no. I'm so sorry. God, how could I have let this happen?" the man groaned again.

St. Scot could hear the faint wail of a siren and at the same moment saw a large Bentley sedan pull into the driveway. Portunoff jumped out from behind the wheel. "Simon, are you all right?" he asked immediately, walking quickly toward St. Scot.

"Yes, Vladimir, I'm fine," said St. Scot.

Portunoff then turned to the guard. "Andy, what happened, are you all right?" There was real concern on the Russian's face.

"Yes, Mr. Portunoff. I'm fine. I'm just so sorry that I let this happen. They jumped me before I knew what was going on. It's all my fault," the guard said, clearly distressed.

The ambulance arrived and a paramedic knelt next to the guard. "Is he the only one hurt?" another emergency worker asked.

St. Scot nodded as Portunoff reassured the guard that it wasn't his fault.

It took the firefighters two hours before the last of the blaze was extinguished. The fire was extremely hot and molten metal fell into rain puddles with a sharp hissing noise. Sections of the roof fell in and then the entire structure finally collapsed.

For St. Scot, whose collection of classic cars had burned to the ground such a short time ago, the experience was all too familiar. The smells from the burning building triggered bad memories.

"This isn't so bad," said Portunoff to St. Scot, as they stood off to one side from the activity.

"How do you mean?" asked St. Scot.

"Well, we were going to have to destroy the copies anyway, and now that Mr. Marshfield has done that for us in such a convincing way, all we have to do is go and get the real cars from where Mr. Filby has been hiding them."

"And do you know where that is? asked St. Scot.

"As it happens, yes I do. Perhaps you will join me this evening? I thought perhaps you might like to be in on this. It should prove interesting," said Portunoff.

St. Scot nodded slowly. "Certainly, Vladimir, anything," he said.

The Russian smiled sadly. "Good, good. But let's hope it doesn't come to that. I need to make preparations. Perhaps you would stay here and speak with the police?" Portunoff then went off, leaving St. Scot to speak with the police, fire departments and arson investigators.

Late in the afternoon, the arson investigator finally asked him if he wanted to examine the wreckage of the burned-out building. The man brought St. Scot through the rubble to the center of the building where the cars had been.

"It's a good thing your friend managed to get the cars out before the fire started," the investigator said amiably.

St. Scot stopped short. "What do you mean?" he asked.

"I heard that they had been storing some really expensive cars in here, so it's good they were gone." The investigator pointed to the place where the roof had completely collapsed. "If the cars had really been here instead of all of those cardboard boxes and piles of steel, nothing would have been left of 'em but scrap metal. It's just a good thing is all I'm saying."

St. Scot looked at the pile of rubble beneath his feet. "Yes, a good thing," he replied, his voice trailing off.

Chapter 28

The rain was still falling from the dark sky when St. Scot met Portunoff that night in front of the Russian's hotel. They got into the Bentley driven by one of his bodyguards. Another of the large bodyguards got into the passenger seat and St. Scot noticed three large men in a Ford Expedition behind them. Portunoff looked tired.

"I have been on the phone to Russia all afternoon," he said. "Many things are happening and I fear tonight will not go as smoothly as I had hoped," Portunoff said sadly. "Mr. Marshfield's employment with WPI has been terminated and I expect he will find it difficult to get any sort of job in the future. He won't be welcome back in Russia anytime soon either."

As they drove away from the manor, St. Scot turned to the Russian. "I just have one question," he said quietly.

Portunoff smiled. "Only one comrade? That's all? Well, what is it then?"

St. Scot chose his words carefully. "Why did you have to burn down my firehouse?"

Portunoff sighed a great sigh and slumped back into the leather seat of the Bentley.

"So you know," he said.

"Yes," said St. Scot.

"Was it my stupid affection for that damn Allard?" the Russian asked.

"It was that, yes, but more. I talked to the arson investigator this afternoon. I suddenly saw the whole plan and realized that only you could have pulled it off," said St. Scot.

"Ah, so you know that part, too?" Portunoff sighed again.

St. Scot ignored the question. "What part of any story you have told me in any of this whole affair has been the truth?" asked St. Scot asked, his voice etched with irritation.

The Russian smiled at him. "Most of it. Some of it. Not much. What part did you believe?" Vladimir asked, still smiling.

"I believed all of it," St. Scot said quietly.

"Good," said Portunoff. "Then that part was true."

"You still haven't answered my question about my firehouse," St. Scot continued.

Portunoff turned to face him. "When you found out my Allard was a fake, I worked fast and found out that Terrance Filby had made other fakes. I saw a chance to make some money, but only if I could get rid of any physical evidence that the cars weren't real. I couldn't be sure how many cars Filby had made and how many of the cars you had worked on and saved the patterns for so I arranged for your firehouse to burn down, taking all of those wooden metal-working patterns and whatever records you had, with it. Pointing your suspicions toward Ivan Blinsky as the arsonist was easy," the Russian admitted.

St. Scot had to ask another question. "What about Terrance Filby?" he said. "Did he really counterfeit all of those cars?"

Portunoff sighed. "Yes. That part is true. I met with Filby again, after you and I had our meeting with him."

The Russian looked pleased with himself.

"I persuaded him, yes, that is the word, I persuaded him that I needed to bring all of the cars together at my warehouse, so that I could replace the counterfeit cars with real ones. That was before I saw all of the cars together. Simon, the cars are all so beautiful, are they not? Anyway, last night my men and I removed the cars from the warehouse and this afternoon I arranged with one of my bodyguards to set fire to the steel building and then he allowed himself to be knocked unconscious. A very loyal man. That was for your benefit. When he awoke, all he had to do was claim he was knocked on the head, you would assume it was Marshfield who did it, and I had my story."

Portunoff leaned further back into the back seat and closed his eyes. St. Scot thought Vladimir might be going to sleep, but he spoke again after a few minutes.

"It was always my plan to take the original cars from Filby and substitute them for the fake ones that I had sold to my comrades in Russia. I needed to do this to make things right with my comrades or I would be in deep trouble because I had sold the Japanese the fake cars in the first place. You understand?"

Portunoff seemed so earnest, but St. Scot wondered how much of *this* story from the spymaster was the truth.

He changed the subject. "Who is Winston Marshfield then?"

Portunoff took a long time in answering.

"A competitor," he said finally. "A rival of mine who I needed to eliminate. Once, he was a comrade. Once, he was in the same business as I. Spy games. For a long time he worked for the other side, for your American government. Then, he worked for us. For KGB. Double agent. It was very useful and he gave us much. After my government fell he continued working for some of us who saw areas where we might profit from what was going on in my country and around the world. Marshfield wanted more than we were willing to give him. We thought we could buy him off by making him a publisher, but a man like that always wants to have more."

St. Scot shook his head. "Vladimir, how much of that story is true?"

Portunoff looked at St. Scot sadly.

"What do you want me to tell you, Simon? That you are working for the good guys? That I am the one with the white hat and Marshfield has a black one? Good and evil? Is that what you want to believe? Life is never that simple."

The Russian stretched his legs out and settled back into the leather upholstery.

"Simon, if you wish I will let you out now. You don't have to be a part of this. It's too late to decide that Marshfield can be reasonable. Too much has happened. If I know Mr. Winston Marshfield," said Portunoff, "and I do know my former comrade, I am sure he will have a little reception for us at Filby's warehouse where we are now going to get the original cars."

A chill went down St. Scot's spine. *What did Portunoff think Marshfield was capable of doing?* The two men rode in silence as the windshield wipers swished the rain from the windshield. Finally St. Scot asked another question.

"So what does Blinsky have to do with all of this?"

Portunoff looked at him for a long moment.

"He works for Marshfield, now at least," the Russian said. "Marshfield ran Blinsky like he was a spy when he was in Austria. He fed Blinsky information about the Russian auto industry to make him look good and then brought him here to take over your magazine." Portunoff smiled again. "That Blinsky really is an idiot. He just doesn't see that Marshfield is using him to run the magazine into the ground so that he can take it away from WPI," the Russian said.

"So that part is true, the part with Filby and the magazine?" asked St. Scot.

"Yes, I am afraid it is true. Filby is actually in way over his head with a guy like Marshfield. He should have stuck with faking cars. Now he is into the WPI mess and the business with Wilden and the money laundering. I am not sure I will be able to save him."

Portunoff now turned again in his seat to face St. Scot and looked troubled.

"He is a wild card, your friend Filby, and I don't know what he will do. In fact, I expect that Filby would be just as happy to get his original cars back and let Marshfield blame their disappearance on Mr. You and Mr. Me."

There was a time when St. Scot would have never believed that his friend Terrance Filby could do such a thing. But now? Now he wasn't so sure.

The Russian sat back again and watched the wipers swish across the Bentley's windscreen.

They traveled for twenty minutes along a rural highway until they came to a dirt road. The rain had stopped and tire tracks of a big truck were still evident in the soft muddy surface. The car came to a chain link fence and a gate. Parked outside the gate was a large enclosed vehicle transport truck without any markings. One man was next to the gate control box and did something and the motor started, sliding the gate open. There was a gravel driveway that went through the trees and the vehicles followed the drive until they arrived at a huge metal storage building. A set of outdoor halogen lights came on, activated by a motion detector. Another few minutes later and the huge roll-up door at the front of the building opened. The driver parked the Bentley outside the building, alongside the Ford Expedition that held Portunoff's men. St. Scot and Portunoff climbed out of the Bentley as the transport truck turned around and backed up to the roll-up door.

St. Scot and Portunoff walked into the building. Inside St. Scot saw the collection of cars he'd thought he'd just seen burn to the ground in the warehouse in the city. The cars were pristine and perfect. And genuine. St. Scot walked straight to the bright red Allard and ran his finger under the fender. He felt three small bumps. This was the original, of that he was sure. *Well, maybe sure. Hell, he wasn't sure of anything anymore!* The men who had ridden over in the Expedition began pushing the first of the genuine racing cars toward the door. The driver of the transport truck opened the rear gate to the vehicle and lowered the ramps into place.

The men pushed the first car, an exquisite blue Bugatti Type 35, into the trailer and forward to the front tie down point. The driver began attaching the chains and straps that would hold the car into place, and the other men walked back into the building and began pushing the next car, a white Mercedes-Benz SSKL, toward the trailer.

The five men were returning from this trip when one of them tripped and fell. A pool of crimson immediately formed next to his head. In the half second it took for the rest of the men to react, another of their number was cut down, shot through the head like the first. The three remaining men screamed a warning as they dove for cover, pulling machine pistols from under their coats and scrambling to find anything they could hide behind. Portunoff reacted fast, grabbing St. Scot and pulling him to safety behind the remaining cars in the garage. Suddenly, the rattle of automatic weapon fire opened into the building, splintering the edge of the truck and sending chips of concrete ricocheting around the inside of the building. Portunoff's guards returned fire and a blue smoke began to drift through the open expanse of the building.

"Mr. Marshfield appears to have found our address," Portunoff said calmly.

St. Scot was anything but calm. He saw everything that was happening at the slow speed of a dream. It was impossible to know how many of the enemy they were facing and to St. Scot the building seemed to have little strategic advantage to hold off a determined force. The driver of the truck had ducked behind the racing cars in his truck and was now holding an automatic pistol in one hand. St. Scot watched as the driver slowly worked his way to the rear of the truck. Lying on his stomach, the man crawled the last few yards to the rear opening and carefully peeked around the corner. This was met with a hail of gunfire that bounced off the side of the truck. As everyone's attention was diverted toward the back of the truck, one of Portunoff's men jumped up and ran through the open door, diving for cover between the huge rear wheels of the truck. From this position he opened fire and there was a muffled cry from outside the building. St. Scot heard the man inside the truck say something in Russian and the man by the rear wheels poured a long burst into the rainy night as the man inside jumped out of the truck. If the attack had come from only one direction he might have made it, but a sudden burst of automatic weapon's fire from the opposite side shot him down. At the same time, another of the men inside the building jumped up and ran out the door, only to be hit by a burst from the same gun.

The battle was going badly. Portunoff and St. Scot were trapped behind the red Allard. The distance between them and the open door made for a perfect killing ground for the gunman outside. One of Portunoff's men remained inside the building, under cover near some barrels, and the other was outside, hiding behind the truck's tires.

"I expect," said Portunoff to St. Scot with amazing calmness, "That our friend Marshfield is moving to a better position so that he can attack us in here. We can't let him do that. Stay here," Portunoff said, jumping up and running toward the other man at the open doorway. The man at the doorway and the one under the truck understood immediately and provided covering fire for their boss. He almost made it, but was hit by a shot that went clear through his shoulder. Portunoff fell to the ground. In an instant, the man by the door jumped up, ran to his boss and dragged him across the floor to safety. He paid a high price for his loyalty as he was hit in the chest just before reaching the relative safety of the barrels, and went down in a heap. The man under the truck poured another long burst into the darkness and one of the automatic weapons suddenly fell silent.

St. Scot reasoned it was just a matter of time now before the men outside would rush the remaining bodyguard and take the building. Portunoff hadn't provided him with any weapon and St. Scot was defenseless crouching behind the Allard. Then he suddenly got an idea. It was reckless and would probably get him killed, but at this rate almost anything he did would have that same end result. St. Scot saw that the right hand drive Allard roadster he was hiding behind was pointing the right direction for him to creep alongside the sports car and up to the driver's door, which is what he did. He opened the door carefully and, crouching low, pulled himself into the seat. Thankfully the key was in the ignition and St. Scot switched it on. Nothing. For an instant he panicked, thinking that maybe the battery was dead or had been removed. Then he remembered that the car had been used for vintage racing and was required to have an electrical cutoff switch. He reached across the cockpit and pulled the red switch handle down.

Immediately the ignition light on the dashboard glowed at him and he heard the ticking of the electrical fuel pump as it pulled fuel from the tank to the huge carburetors atop the Cadillac V-8 engine. St. Scot prayed during the seconds it took for the clattering of the pump to subside, indicating that there was fuel in the tank. Crouching ever lower, he checked that the manual transmission was in neutral and then hit the starter button. The big V-8 cranked lazily before suddenly booming into life. The open racing exhausts made a huge noise inside the enclosed space of the metal building and St. Scot saw the man under the truck look into the building with astonishment. St. Scot sat up suddenly, pushed the heavy clutch pedal to the floor and pushed the stubby chrome shift lever into first gear. He slipped the clutch and with the rear tires squealing slid the car through an arc that would take him to the front door.

The first burst of gunfire came through the warehouse door and missed the car narrowly, sending up puffs of concrete dust as it stitched a line next to the roaring racer. St. Scot slid to a stop next to the open door and while the man under the truck fired a covering burst, St. Scot jumped out of the car and ran around to the other side to Portunoff. The Russian was still alive and groaned heavily as St. Scot dragged him to the passenger side of the car and pushed his bulk into the cockpit. Just then another rain of gunfire came through the open door and smashed the passenger side aero screen windshield. St. Scot ducked low and ran back to the other side of the idling car. He dove into the car, rammed it into first and stood on the throttle. *Too much!* The rear wheels spun with the car's massive torque and the car jumped sideways. A hail of bullets rattled against the front of the car and St. Scot was glad to have the cast iron engine block of the mammoth Caddy V-8 up front to absorb the impacts. The Allard slid out of the building and St. Scot pulled up behind the truck just as the remaining guard stood and emptied his gun in the direction of a black sport utility vehicle, behind which were crouched two of the men that were firing at the Allard. Both men screamed and their guns were silent. St. Scot turned to urge the man to jump onto the tail of the car, just in time to see him suddenly stumble forward as gunshots came from the other side of the compound.

St. Scot hesitated an instant before realizing that he could do nothing for the dying man. Slamming the throttle to the floor he again spun the rear wheels and, sliding sideways, drove around the truck and headed for the front gate. Bullets tore into the rear bodywork of the car and several smashed some of the instruments on the dashboard. As he left the lights of the compound he realized he couldn't see where he was going. He flipped a switch on the dash and the right headlight illuminated, the left one having been shot out. The rain was now lashing into his eyes and blurring his vision. He felt around the cockpit and found an old set of aviator's goggles slung around the gear shift lever. Working them over his head he pulled them into place. At least he could now see.

The wooden dash in front of him splintered and suddenly St. Scot felt a searing hot pain in his side, just below his left armpit. *They were still shooting at him.* He reached under his arm and felt warm sticky blood. He almost fainted from the pain and the shock of being shot but the cold rain helped keep him lucid. The gravel road turned ahead just before the gate and it came up so quickly that it caught St. Scot by surprise. The big car began to slide and St. Scot applied opposite lock and a bit of throttle. It was no use, he was going to hit the trees on the side of the road. The rear of the car grazed a few small bushes and then smacked hard into a medium sized oak tree. St. Scot stalled the engine and for an instant there was complete silence. Then he heard a car near the building start and quickly he reached for the Allard's starter button. The big Caddy engine burst into life again. St. Scot spun the rear wheels but they were caught in the ditch on the side of the road. He quickly slammed the car into reverse and the car lurched backward a foot. He slid the gearshift into first and fed the power more gently this time and the sports car climbed the depression of the ditch and headed down the gravel road toward the open gate. Behind him, in the rear view mirror that had been partially splintered by a crashing bullet, he could see the lights of a car taking up chase.

The car in the yard next to Filby's building had been a new Lexus sedan, a more powerful version of last year's edition that St. Scot had liked so much. The Allard St. Scot was driving might have been one of the fastest and most fearsome racing cars of its day, but that day was 1952. A lot of progress had been made in automotive engineering in fifty years and the new Lexus sedan almost immediately had caught up to the tail of the Allard. St. Scot reached the end of the dirt road and turned the sports car onto the highway. As he made the turn he looked in the mirror and suddenly had a tiny glimmer of hope. Driving the car was Ivan Rachmaninov Blinsky! The same Ivan Blinsky who had so comprehensively demonstrated to St. Scot his complete lack of driving ability back on the frozen lake in Norway. *Maybe he had a chance.* His moment of hope was shattered, however, when two more shots hit the wooden dashboard, not an inch away from his left hand on the Allard's wood-rimmed steering wheel. Looking back, St. Scot could see Winston Marshfield standing on the passenger seat next to Blinsky in the big luxury sedan, taking aim with a pistol through the car's open sunroof. A wave of nausea hit St. Scot as he realized his entire left side was now soaked in blood. He was having trouble breathing and as he swerved the Allard from side to side to ruin Marshfield's aim, the heavy steering of the old sports car made him feel like there was a dagger being twisted between his ribs.

Simon knew that, as quick as the Lexus was, it wasn't a sports car and he intended to use that knowledge to his best advantage. Rapidly approaching a series of bends, instead of braking, he threw the Allard into a long slide, hoping to mislead Blinsky into taking the corner too fast. The Lexus dropped back a bit, but was tracking through the corner with amazing surefootedness. *Of course!* The Lexus had a computerized dynamic stability system that read the slip at each wheel and then selectively applied individual brakes to keep the car from sliding off the road. The high-technology system could make even a ham-fisted idiot like Blinsky look like Mario Andretti. St. Scot stood on the throttle and the Allard jumped ahead briefly on brute acceleration, but the higher top speed of the Lexus soon brought the luxury sedan back within easy range of the vintage sports car.

Another couple of shots plowed into the rounded tail of the Allard. The engine of the sports car suddenly began to run roughly and St. Scot looked in horror at the temperature gauge. Its needle was climbing past 230 degrees. The radiator must have been hit when they made their escape. The car would soon overheat and grind to a stop as the engine seized. St. Scot's vision was beginning to tunnel down and darken at the edges. His breathing was becoming more and more difficult and he felt lightheaded. The Lexus was right on his tail again and another shot screamed past his ear and shattered the aero screen in front of him. Shards of glass cut into his face but his eyes were protected by the aviator's goggles. Behind him, Marshfield was standing up again in the passenger seat of the Lexus and his aim was getting deadly. Ahead, St. Scot could see the rain soaked road made a curve to the right.

His options were running out and the pain in his left side had become almost unbearable. Something inside told him that this might be his last chance to throw off his pursuers. Never lifting his foot from the throttle he threw the Allard into the right-hand bend. The Dunlop racing tires held at first and then started sliding inexorably to the outside of the turn. The car was in a four-wheel drift when it hit the wet grass and immediately the rear slid out into a lurid slide. The car was now fully sideways and heading for a stand of stout trees. At the last possible instant, St. Scot saw a small logging trail on the left heading into the woods. He lifted his foot from the throttle suddenly, to unbalance the car, and then threw the steering wheel over to cause the sports car to pendulum in the opposite direction, while feeding power back to the rear wheels. The move worked and the car shot up the logging trail, missing several large trees by inches. Behind him, he saw headlights swinging wildly and then heard a loud crash. St. Scot hit the brakes hard and brought the Allard to a stop. The logging trail was a dead end and now he was trapped. Desperately, he looked back at the Lexus and realized it was sitting motionless. He didn't know how long he sat there, waiting for something to happen, but nothing did. Shaking, but with no other option, he found reverse and slowly backed the Allard until it was even with the Lexus. Although the stability control system of the Lexus could do wonders, it couldn't beat the laws of physics. Blinsky had hit the grass and then overshot the little dirt road and had run straight into a medium sized tree. Marshfield, who had been standing in the open sunroof had been catapulted through the air and had hit the tree. He was lying on the hood of the crumpled Lexus with his head split open like a melon. Both front airbags had deployed in the crash and Blinsky was sitting slumped and unmoving against the steering wheel.

St. Scot felt unconnected to the rest of his body, but managed to reverse onto the main road and continue onward at a slow speed. His head was gradually being enveloped in darkness and all he wanted to do was to close his eyes for a moment and rest. He vaguely recognized where he was: not far from Terrance Filby's place. He pointed the Allard in that direction and pressed on the gas pedal. Suddenly he was on the drive to Filby's and the car climbed the three steps to the front porch before crashing through the front door of the house. St. Scot saw a grief stricken Barbara Filby coming down the main hallway and for a brief instant before everything went dark he wondered: *Would she cry at his funeral?*

CHAPTER 29

There was an annoying hissing noise. St. Scot tried to raise his arm and swat whatever insect was causing this irritation, except he couldn't raise his arm. His eyes felt glued together but he had to open them to make the hissing sound stop. With great willpower, he forced his left eye to open. The glare from the white wall and white sheets was awful. He squinted and tried to open his right eye. The view there was better. It was of Detective Linda Jameson and she was smiling and crying all at the same time. Slowly he shook his head and his slightly blurry vision seemed to clear. It *was* Linda and he was suddenly aware that she was holding his hand. His throat was raw and sore and he wanted something to drink. Jameson was pushing a button on the bed and the room soon filled with nurses. Eventually a resident showed up and explained that the breathing tube they had used was the reason for his sore throat and certainly he could have a drink of water.

As soon as he was able to talk, and he was alone again with Jameson, he asked her to tell him where he was and how he had gotten there.

She said, "You drove the Allard through Terrance Filby's front door. You and the man you were with, Vladimir Portunoff, were both unconscious and covered with blood. Barbara Filby immediately called an ambulance and the police."

He squeezed her hand and she squeezed back.

She paused and took a breath. "Barbara and Terrance Filby decided to get you out of the car. Vladimir, Mr. Portunoff, had a huge wound in his shoulder but at first they couldn't find where you had been hit. Your breathing was very bad and then they noticed the wound under your left arm. It took forever, but two ambulances finally arrived and took you and Vladimir to the hospital. They radioed ahead that you had a broken rib, collapsed lung and had lost lots of blood. The doctors brought you into the emergency room, gave you a blood transfusion, and patched up your lung. The loss of blood had us all pretty worried and you've been drifting in and out of consciousness for four days."

"What day is it?" St. Scott suddenly asked.

"It's Thursday, you've been in here since Sunday night," she answered.

St. Scot was afraid to ask the next question. "What about Vladimir, is he going to be all right?"

Jameson squeezed St. Scot's hand as she explained Portunoff's case.

"The bullet that caught Mr. Portunoff in the shoulder passed cleanly through his scapula before exiting out his back. Although he lost a fair amount of blood, he was in much better shape than you. On Monday night that old Russian bastard friend of yours had himself discharged from the hospital to the care of his private physician. Then, against the orders of the police department, he had a private jet fly him directly to England where he said they would take better care of him. I saw him just before he left the hospital and he told me that he had arranged it so that you would have whatever you needed to get well."

"You saw him? You met Vladimir?" St. Scot asked.

"Yes, I met him. Charming man. Delightful. He told me things about you that you probably don't want me to know," she said with a smile.

"You mustn't believe what Vladimir tells you. He is a consummate liar," St. Scot said.

"What about Ivan Blinsky?" asked St. Scot, suddenly remembering him slumped against the steering wheel of the Lexus. "Was he badly injured in the crash?"

"Marshfield was dead when the police discovered the car. They say he flew out of the sunroof and hit a tree. Blinsky was dead, too. It's a weird thing. The guys on the force said that the safety systems in the Lexus would have kept him alive, but apparently when Marshfield flew out of the sunroof, the gun he was holding in his hand had been pointing downward and went off just as he left the car. The bullet caught Blinsky in the top of the head and killed him instantly."

St. Scot was feeling very tired but suddenly remembered Jameson's injury.

"What's the matter," she asked, noticing St. Scot's sudden look of concern.

"How are you? You saved my life and almost died yourself," he said quietly.

"Well, I guess I'll be off work for a few weeks. Apparently I was lucky, another quarter inch in and the bullet would have killed me. As it is, your quick first aid made all the difference. So it seems you saved my life, too, so I guess we're even."

"Are you in trouble with your boss?" St. Scot asked.

"Yeah, probably," she said. "Captain Saunders told me it's a good thing I got shot, or he would have to be pretty tough on me. They really frown on it when you date suspects, or even former suspects," she said with a smile.

They sat quietly holding hands.

Slowly St. Scot's drugged brain worked out something that still bothered him.

"Which Allard was it?" he asked.

Jameson didn't seem to understand the question. "The car you drove through the front door, you mean? That's strange," Jameson answered. "It disappeared from the front steps sometime early the next morning. Nobody knows where the car has gone and my pals on the force are furious. I expect you'll be seeing them later."

St. Scot was now feeling very sleepy. But he needed to ask one more question. "What about the men who were killed at the warehouse?" he said groggily.

Jameson looked puzzled and before she could say anything, St. Scot fell asleep.

The next morning, St. Scot awoke, clear-headed and feeling stiff in his ribs. He carefully ate his hospital breakfast of French toast and orange juice. He thought sadly about how much the hospital's French toast would have been improved with just a hint of cinnamon. Looking around for the first time, he noticed his room had several new baskets of flowers. One had a get-well card signed by Allison, Amanda and Ronnie. The biggest bunch of flowers had a card from Elizabeth Meyers that said, *I'm sorry, I was wrong. Please forgive me.*

After his breakfast, the police paid him a visit. They wanted to know more about the bullet-riddled Allard, where it had gone, how St. Scot and Portunoff had been shot, and why Blinsky and Marshfield had driven into a tree. Portunoff hadn't told them anything before he left apparently so St. Scot was trying to be as vague as possible. The sergeant in charge threatened to charge St. Scot with withholding evidence, but since he had been unconscious in the hospital when the Allard disappeared, it was clearly an idle threat. The police didn't ask him any questions about the shootout at Portunoff's warehouse, so St. Scot was able to keep quiet about that, too.

A short time after they left, Terrance Filby walked into St. Scot's hospital room. Coming up to the bed, Filby patted St. Scot on his shoulder.

"Glad to hear you're going to make it," he said. "You had us all a bit worried for a little while there. Barbara sends her love and told me to tell you she promises to come and visit you tomorrow."

"I'm surprised to see you," said St. Scot.

"What are friends for?" Filby answered, looking at St. Scot for a few moments before sitting down in the chair next to the bed.

"I don't know how to say this, so I'll say it straight out," St. Scot began. "You could have let Vladimir and me die on your front porch. All you had to do was waste some time calling the ambulance and we probably wouldn't have made it. I'm glad you didn't, but why didn't you?"

Filby shook his head. "Simon, I am a lot of things, but I'm no murderer. The real truth is that I've screwed up. The fake cars and the WPI thing. I was greedy and wanted more."

"Okay," began St. Scot, "Terry, what happened to the cars?"

Filby paused for a second. "Simon, I'll tell you what I can but, honestly, I don't know. The cars that burned up in Portunoff's warehouse were the forgeries I'd made. The real cars were the ones that I had in my warehouse. At least I hope so. I'm assuming that Portunoff has returned the real cars to the rightful owners. But, I don't know for sure. All I'm sure of is that my warehouse is empty now too." Filby looked sad. "Look, I know that what I did was wrong. But imagine if you can what it felt like for me to own all of those really amazing cars. Portunoff knows. He had all of them in one place, even if only for a while. Now, he's the only one who knows for sure that the real cars have gone to their Russian owners. I doubt you will ever get a straight answer out of that crafty fellow."

St. Scot didn't know what to think. The cars, the deception, the fire fight at the warehouse.

"Terry," St. Scot asked finally, "what do you think it was really all about?"

Filby looked uncomfortable.

"I think," he finally answered slowly, "that there were two very powerful men who had strong ties to Russia. Now there is one. I also think our friend Vladimir is much more, um, connected than he let on. This is just a hunch, but I think Marshfield was biting off more than he realized when he decided to eliminate Portunoff. And none of us know what happened exactly with you and Portunoff when the two of you drove the Allard through my front door. Portunoff wouldn't tell us anything and you don't remember."

St. Scot stayed silent.

"I have some other news," Filby said suddenly. "First of all, Mort Welsh is going to go to Japan to work for Vladimir in his Tokyo operation. He'll be working under a Miss Itagaki, as I understand, to help with the high end restorations they do there."

St. Scot thought of the voracious Tamara Itagaki and felt a momentary pang of jealousy.

"I hope he brings a case of Viagra," St. Scot muttered under his breath.

Filby didn't appear to hear him.

"Meanwhile," Filby went on, "I've been asked by Vladimir to replace Winston Marshfield." St. Scot looked up quickly. "I know what you're thinking. That I'm the last person who should get that job. Well, maybe so, but just maybe I can make something good happen, too."

St. Scot figured it was Portunoff's way of paying the man off for the collection of original cars that Filby had lost, and for his continued silence about the forgeries.

"After you've had a chance to think about it, Simon, I want you to consider coming back to your old job at the magazine. Actually, I want you to take my old job and be in charge. You're really the only person I trust in that position and you'll have a lot to do to fix the mess that Blinsky left behind." There was some irony for St. Scot that Blinsky had made the very mess of things that Filby and Marshfield had wanted him to make.

"And the money laundering?" St. Scot continued, wanting every answer.

"Oh, you know about that too? Well, that's in the past. Wilden has been indicted for insider trading and it's pretty clear that

WPI won't be dealing with him anymore. At least not if I have anything to say about it," said Filby.

"And what about Bill Borgenson?" Simon asked quietly.

Filby's eyes clouded for an instant. "If only Bill had kept his mouth shut."

Suddenly there didn't seem to be much for the pair to talk about.

"I can see you're getting tired," Filby said, getting up from his chair. "I'll come by and see you again, if that would be okay."

St. Scot gave Filby a wan smile. It was true. He was tired. Tired of everything that had gone on.

"Sure, that'd be fine." He managed to say and watched as Filby turned and left. That evening, after Jameson had visited and left, St. Scot's bedside telephone rang. It was Portunoff calling from London. The Russian sounded healthy and cheerful and assured St. Scot that he was receiving the best possible care from his own private doctor.

"I underestimated the firepower that Marshfield could bring to the party. For that I am sorry."

Even over the phone St. Scot could imagine the Russian's expressive face.

"Anyway, during the shootout, before I was shot, I had called for reinforcements on my cell phone, but they got there too late to help you dispose of Mr. Marshfield and Mr. Blinsky the way you did, and in such a professional manner." Portunoff's tone brightened. "When the other of my men finally arrived after we had escaped, they found the rest of the original cars and loaded them into the transport truck. So, you see, it all worked out. And you were worried." said the Russian.

"Where is the Allard?" St. Scot asked.

Portunoff chuckled. "Which Allard was that?" he asked. "There have been so many I have started to lose track."

St. Scot was feeling confused again and, after all he'd been through, slightly irritated.

"Vladimir, tell me truthfully, are you going to return the original cars or the forgeries?" asked St. Scot.

There was a long pause and then a sigh and then Portunoff changed the subject.

"Simon, there is something I want you to do for me, well, for me and for WPI. We want you as publisher of your old magazine and also to oversee the creation of a new automotive group. I want you to know you will have complete control and I promise I won't interfere, even if you say bad things."

St. Scot didn't know what to say. *A shot at the big time in publishing? He would be a fool to refuse the job. Was this Portunoff's way of keeping him quiet about the forgeries?*

"I thought you were giving that job to Filby," said St. Scot.

"Hmm? No, he would be your boss and you would run the automotive end," replied Portunoff.

Still, it was a hell of an offer. But did he want to move to New York now, with the possibility of a relationship with Jameson? *Would she move?* Vladimir seemed to read his mind.

"You can locate your headquarters anyplace you want to and to take some time before you make your decision."

Throughout this whole episode, St. Scot had been a pawn used by powerful men. It was clear that, as much as he liked Vladimir Portunoff, the Russian had probably never once told him the truth. That, and the man had some fairly nefarious friends, some of whom owned WPI. These were people who had no compunctions about demolishing the lines between advertising and editorial, or between life and death. Did he really want to become involved again with people to whom human life seemed so cheap and everyone was for sale if the price was high enough? He thought of poor Bill Borgenson. If St. Scot didn't do what was required would he, too, find an early grave? The truth was that his friend Vladimir Portunoff had enough power to make all that had happened occur: to burn down his warehouse, to end up with both the forgeries and the originals, and to make the bodies of all of those others killed in the shootout disappear. No matter how much he liked the man personally, St. Scot knew that the Russian was dangerous—too dangerous.

"I'll think about it, Vladimir," St. Scot said before he rang off, but he knew he wouldn't. Dangerous or not, would he really want to work for someone who never even thanked him for saving his life? *Petty? Maybe. But you had to draw the line somewhere.*

The next morning there was a knock on St. Scot's hospital room door. It was pushed open by Elizabeth Meyers. She was dressed with casual weekend elegance, tailored in silk and smiling at St. Scot. "Want some company?" she said simply, as she pulled up the bedside chair.

"I got your card," St. Scot managed to say, slightly irritated with himself that he was so pleased to see her.

"I'm sorry that I doubted you, Simon. I should have known better. I should have remembered who you were and known that you would never be involved in these types of things." She took his hand. "Do you think you can forgive me for being a fool?"

He felt the warmth of her hand and the soft look in her eyes. "Yes, Elizabeth. I do forgive you. I know that whatever information they brought to you must have been convincing. Let's just leave it at that and remain friends, okay?"

Elizabeth smiled at St. Scot. "Maybe more than friends? How would you like to come and work for me? I still haven't filled that job on my staff, and I sure would like to have you with me…"

"Are you trying to tempt me to the dark side, again, Elizabeth?" he asked.

She laughed her rich, deep laugh, tossing her head back so that her auburn hair fell back on her shoulders. "Yes, I guess I am, Simon. Just take some time and think about it. There will always be a place for you…"

The next afternoon, the hospital finally discharged St. Scot. Linda Jameson was there to take him home. They made quite the convalescing couple. The dressing on her neck had been reduced to a large square white bandage. His left arm was in a sling and was taped across his body. Movement was fairly painful for him, although the doctors promised he would have a full recovery.

Jameson helped him into the passenger side of his pickup truck. Her Miata would have been too difficult and besides, thanks to his outstanding marksmanship, it still needed a new windshield—a fact that she continually teased him about.

Once they were on the road, St. Scot realized they weren't heading out of town toward the farm but, instead, in the direction of his firehouse. When they pulled up out front, he saw that the exterior work had been finished and it looked better than new. How could they have finished it all so quickly? *Portunoff! The man had influence almost everywhere.*

Jameson helped him from the car and he leaned on her as they walked together to the big front doors. She pulled out a key and opened the door and, with his good arm, he reached in to hit the lights. The inside of the building was wonderful, better than it had been before the fire. The workman had obviously put in a lot of overtime to get everything finished and the result was breathtaking. And there, in the center of the floor, was something even more breathtaking.

It was a 1931 Duesenberg Limousine, shimmering black with a gaudy red interior. *It seemed that Portunoff had figured out a way to say thank you after all.*

With Jameson's help, St. Scot walked stiffly up to the car and let his hand run along the seductive curve of its fender. The last time he had seen this car had been in Tokyo, with Miss Itagaki, and the big car's windows had been steamed. Jameson looked at him quizzically and St. Scot turned, carefully took her in his free arm and asked her quietly,

"I don't suppose you know anything about Tallulah Bankhead?"

About the Author—

Kevin Clemens has been a part of the automotive industry for more than 25 years. Trained as an engineer, he worked as a research scientist, designer of racing and sports car tires and public relations counselor. He has been an editor and contributor at some of the industry's most influential automotive enthusiast magazines. He has written extensively about everything from racing vintage sports cars to the most sophisticated automotive technologies. As a magazine staffer and freelance writer, he knows the life of the automotive journalist from the inside.

In 2005, his collection of automotive essays, *Motor Oil For a Car Guy's Soul*, received the Ken Purdy Award for Excellence in Automotive Journalism. Clemens lives in Lake Elmo, Minnesota, with his wife and a pair of Australian Shepherds, one of which is certified for wilderness search and rescue. *Eat Free or Die* is his first novel.